HER

HER

By Malachi Bailey

Copyright © 2019 Malachi Bailey

All rights reserved. No part of this publication may be reproduced, distributed, or transmitted in any form or by any means, without prior written permission from the author except brief excerpts for review purposes.

Her/Malachi Bailey. -- 1st ed.

ISBN: 9781530919291

Mother One Publications
http://motheronepublications.com
www.facebook.com/MalachitheWriter/

Dedication

I dedicate *Her* to my late, loving mother, Debra Ann Hines. Mommy, you knew I was an author before I did! Thank you for always encouraging me to write and share my stories. I'll always remember you would drop everything just to hear my latest story. So, my debut novel is for you!

Love always, your firstborn, Malachi.

Contents

Dedication 5
Chapter 1 9
Chapter 2 11
Chapter 3 13
Chapter 4 17
Chapter 5 29
Chapter 6 39
Chapter 7 49
Chapter 8 55
Chapter 9 65
Chapter 10 81
Chapter 11 95
Chapter 12 109
Chapter 13 125
Chapter 14 149
Epilogue 1 157
Epilogue 2 163
Acknowledgements 167

1

> "It is far harder to kill a phantom than a reality."
> --Virginia Woolf, *The Death of the Moth and Other Essays*

Time. There is never enough time. And yet, it can stretch out before you like a long, winding road with no end in sight. The same can be said about life. And if you had a life like hers, well, you would understand.

She felt as if she had seen it all. And perhaps she had. The days, the weeks, the years, the endless march of centuries seemed to roll into one. The people, the clothing, the ideals, the dynasties . . . all lived and died in a blink of an eye.

She was getting ahead of herself, which was often the case whenever she was in the realm of waiting, the in between. Reflecting on memories and lives that had closed like chapters in a book. Those memories and the accompanying sensations, so cherished and endearing, stayed with her like sugar melting on her tongue. She had formed connections and bonds with the most remarkable people. Equal parts angels and demons in the guise of humans. Sometimes, she could not tell the difference. They served a purpose, played the role destiny deigned for them. She learned from them and, most importantly, remembered them. Mental replay as she drifted in the void of endless dreaming. She would have smiled if she could. If she had lips.

A myriad of impossible colors swirled around her, through her. Where did it end? Where did she begin? It was a seamless blend. It merged with her soul, painted it in incandescent shades and hues, leaving streamers of time and memory.

If ever there was the embodiment of living memory, the closest thing to the sum of human experience, then she was it. Not much escaped her watchful eye. It was what she had been bred to do. Her destiny, as it were. From the staccato beat of African drums to animated dubstep tracks in clubs across the country, she was there. She recalled.

Simply . . . her.

There was no forgetting in that realm. They say time and thought are one. And she was always thinking, always learning, for there was no end to that. She was a traveler waiting for her next destination. It was almost time. It happened so fast—the change. Familiar and welcoming. A new life, infantile and reachable. Then crippling, soul-searing pain. Claws ripped at her mind, shredded her sanity. Her lungs filled. Living should not have hurt like that. She surrendered to the miasma of agony that stopped at nothing to unmake her.

2

She remembered dying but not living. It made no sense. She remembered being airborne, the wind whistling though her ears as gravity no longer defied her, the banner of her tresses buoyed by the wind. Was she bleeding? Something hot and wet leaked from various cuts across her body. Yes, it was blood.

She was dying.

The sensation of free fall. Then, just as quickly as it started, it ended. Painfully! Her body hit the surface of cresting waves. The pain was quick as gravity greedily tried to claim her once more. It was working. Bone-chilling cold nipped at her pores before seeping in. Did she splash around? Did she grasp for purchase? She did not remember. Foamy salt water rushed through her mouth and nose, filled her lungs, supplanting the oxygen. An intense scorching sensation accompanied the life-stealing fluid rushing to fill her chest cavity.

Indescribable pressure emanated from her core and sent tendrils of agony through her flailing form. It pulsed in rhythm with her heart, which slammed against her ribcage like a caged beast. Drowning was not quick. It hurt more than anything. Incoherent thoughts swam through her throbbing head. She saw flashes of red and felt herself sinking lower. Distorted light above the waves grew dimmer. The sun had forsaken her. There was only pain exploding in her chest. A tendril of blood spiraled up from her nose, seemingly in slow motion. She watched it twist and turn in the ocean's murky depths. The pressure was crushing her from the inside out.

A kaleidoscope of images blossomed in the ruin of her brain. Death by seconds. How had it come to this? Why did she have to die? Why her? The twinkling light became hazy, soon to become dim and then nothing at all. The ocean's murky depths were on the verge of claiming yet another of its countless victims. Its bottom thousands of leagues below, a graveyard for the wronged, the unfortunate, and the doomed. Would she be yet another ill-fated jewel on that maritime crown?

She could almost see it as she began to lose the strength to fight, the will to live. Lactic acid burned in her arms and legs. Pain exploded all over as the urge to open her mouth hammered against her like the crushing waves that greedily sucked the life from her. In her mind's eye, she saw the half-submerged bones of murdered or traitorous pirates. Slaves stolen from Africa's Gold Coast, shackled together in death as in life. Shipwrecks still home to a treasure trove of exotic jewels. And just a little deeper, the remains of prehistoric marine life that was triple the size of its modern sea-dwelling progeny. And deeper still?

And as her heart slowed, she stopped thrashing her suddenly heavy limbs. The sweet purity of oblivion obscured the edges of her receding vision. The coil of blood dissolved into nothing. She, too, would be the same.

A welcoming darkness claimed the woman with no name.

3

The young man wanted to be somewhere. Anywhere but home, where he had left behind a life that was determined to put him in the grave—figuratively and literally. Too much had happened, and this . . . this was better.

His name was Cyrus Dhandi. All that mattered was the forgetting. Just a fisherman now. He chuckled ruefully to himself. To move on with one's future, one had to forget his past. Or something like that. He could not be bothered to recall the exact quote.

The salt spray sprinkled his face like a fine mist. He closed his eyes to it. *Peaches* swayed under his feet, but he did not care. As long as he was in motion. Getting away. Getting away from it all. He was a long way from his home, which was in the United States. It had been a year since he had cashed out his savings account and taken off for parts unknown.

Now he was in Australia. Cairns, to be exact. The other side of the world. Pulling his weight on a small shrimp trawler each day. Long, exhausting days of routine and repetition. It took some getting used to, life aboard the outrigger trawler and learning the ins and outs of his new trade. The crew was cool to him at first, but over the time, friendships blossomed. One couldn't spend that much time with others under such circumstances and not develop at least a glimmer of camaraderie. Brothers in arms as they pulled life from the sea to sustain theirs.

He was just another guy, another fisherman, and the day was on its way to becoming just like any other day. Until . . .

It was a dry season. Early July. Hot, humid days that cooled considerably by evening. But that night it stormed as if the sky had something personal against the trawler and its crew, hurling buckets of pelting rain and buffeting them with howling winds. The crew had just finished trawling before the clouds darkened, and thunder crackled in the distance. Showers were frequent even during the dry season, but this one was different. Unnerving. Waves pummeled *Peaches*, crashing into her like angry bullies.

Cyrus braced himself against the railing, worried he might fall over the side. "What the hell is going on?" he exclaimed to a fellow fisherman as the man ran past.

The other guy (Zach, was it?) stopped briefly, eyes narrowed against the drenching rain, and cupped his hands around his bearded mouth. "Not sure! Just bad weather! Get below where it's safe!" He hurried off before Cyrus could reply.

Somewhere safe? Out here? Not likely.

It was not their first squall. It was the nature of the business. Yet this one was strange. It was the prickling of his neck hairs standing at full attention. The sensation of feeling someone watching him, but when he turned around, no one was there. The promise of something on the cusp of happening. The sudden urge to fight or flee.

Then there was the water.

"Holy sh—"

Trinity Inlet surged with churning, foaming waves, a scene straight out of *Moby Dick*. Waterspouts descended from the heavens like heralds of the gods—wrathful and with deadly purpose.

Cyrus was transfixed, rooted to the spot. He squinted at the wind that tried its best to send him airborne. A whirlpool materialized in the distance, much too close for his liking. For the first time since childhood, he feared for his life. This was going to be his last day on Earth.

Lights. He saw lights below the choppy waves. Despite his better judgment, he leaned over the railing, eyes narrowed and searching. The crack of thunder resonated deep in his bones. Lightning stitched across the sky in a jagged line. Excitement sprang from the depths of his being, mingled with fear. Something was coming. And beneath the sound of the howling winds, the crashing waves, and the relentless rain, was that the chittering of cicadas in the distance?

Maybe it was his imagination, but what he saw next was undeniably real. A mermaid? No. A woman? Yes, a woman had just surfaced. It was as if the whirlpool had operated in reverse, spitting her out. Once it did, it quickly subsided. Waterspouts still danced in Cyrus's line of vision, but, like the whirlpool, they were no longer as intense and, thankfully, not life-threatening. And yet the woman was still very much drowning!

Thought and action were one. Cyrus dove into the cold, unwelcoming waters like a man possessed. Temporarily disoriented, he quickly spotted the reason for his daring rescue. He kicked his legs as he swam toward her. Beneath the waves, time seemed to slow down. He could see her clearly. Eyes closed. Dark skin. Wavy hair billowing around her. Naked. A tattoo pulsing on her chest. A phoenix and an ankh merged together. There was no time to marvel. He needed to relieve his searing lungs. He encircled her waist with one arm and swam toward the surface.

Later, he swore that once he made contact, he glimpsed a smile on the silent siren's lips.

4

Darkness. An old friend. Always there, always lurking, always comforting. Its soothing blindness. Its velvet veil a retreat from a world that had spat her out. Again? It spoke to her, claimed her, nursed her. Enfolded her like a blanket, blending with her insubstantial form, almost taking her to the realm. Finally. There was no tether. An anchor had no meaning there. Just a speck in the vast sea of nothingness.

Then something happened.

The darkness began to recede. Light played at the edges of her vision. A horizontal line bisected her sight. It wavered for a moment then blinked in and out of existence, the worm of glowing intensity becoming more prevalent. She was being beckoned, summoned back from the void. This purgatory, this lingering non-death, would have to wait.

Life was calling.

She answered.

Eyelids fluttered. A soft exhalation of relief. She opened her eyes.

"Thought you were determined to leave us," a masculine voice said, low, deep, and no doubt bearing an undercurrent of uneasy concern.

She groaned softly and then pushed herself up on her elbows. Silent, she took in her surroundings. She was in a ship's cabin, and judging by the way the room swayed, they were still at sea. Blinking, she positioned herself so her back was against the wall.

She looked down and realized she was wearing an oversized T-shirt. She peeked under the sheets and saw she was also wearing loose-fitting pants. She flushed. Who had dressed her? This man?

For the first time, she truly looked at him. Even in the dim light, she could make out his features. Olive skin that seemed to glow in that setting. Scruff bordering on a beard. His tall frame was seated in a chair beside her. He was bent over, elbows atop his knees, at the side of her bed. Deep-set green eyes, piercing and intense with worry, drank her in. It made her uncomfortable, so she averted her gaze.

"Are you alright?" he asked intently, every trace of his good-humored relief gone. He had an accent, though she could not place it just yet.

She pursed her lips, cleared her throat, and made eye contact once more. "I feel . . . better. Just very thirsty."

She was aware of how rusty her voice sounded. In truth, she barely recognized it. But then she could not remember the last time she had spoken. *Was it really that long ago?*

"I'm not even sure what happened. A lot of it is . . . I don't know . . . hard to recall."

Her host let out another sigh as his shoulders sagged and he broke eye contact. "Honestly, I'm still trying to figure it out myself. I've never seen anything like it. I've . . . I've never saved a life. It was all so crazy."

She raised an eyebrow. "You saved my life?"

It was his turn to blush. He looked at her and then found something incredibly interesting on his leg. "Yeah. I guess I did."

"Oh." She crossed her arms over her chest and cleared her throat again. "Thank you, uh . . . what's your name?"

He looked up, and a warm grin spread across his face. Pride filled his eyes. "Oh yeah. Um, my name is Cyrus. Cyrus Dhandi." He leaned over to shake her hand. "What's your name?"

The woman opened her mouth to speak but then closed it. She tried again. Confusion darkened her features. "I . . . I . . . I don't know."

****

Cyrus had been vigilant as she slept. The last few hours had been hectic and nerve-wracking after they were both brought on board following the freak storm. He remembered sitting there, breathing hard as the crew checked him over, but his only concern was for the mysterious woman he had plucked from the sea. The medic was trying to resuscitate her, to no avail. His hands pumped her chest before he breathed air into her unresponsive lungs. It was madness aboard *Peaches*. The crew was brimming with excitement, running back and forth, trying desperately to return to their former state of normality. Those who were not assigned to a task hovered over Cyrus, the medic, and the woman. Such anticipation had never been felt before. Then, on the third try, the medic's efforts bore fruit.

The woman awoke with a violent jolt. Water gushed from her bloated lips and sprayed the deck. Suddenly, her deep, harsh gasps were all that could be heard. A collective sigh of relief was felt by all. Someone handed Cyrus a robe. He stared at it dumbly for a second and then turned back to the naked woman. *Oh . . . right.*

He rushed over and quickly dressed her. Her tattoo caught his eye again, the phoenix and an ankh entwined together. Interesting. Upon closer inspection, Cyrus noticed it was glowing faintly. Or was it? He blinked. His eyes were playing tricks on him. He looked up and saw everyone staring at him, eyebrows raised in amusement. Why were they staring? Then it dawned upon him. Humiliation sent a wave of warmth throughout his body. *They think I'm about to eat her alive. I can't deal with this right now!*

"It's not like that!"

"Yeah, yeah, sure."

"No, really, it isn't. I thought there was something on her . . . on her . . ." Cyrus dared another peek, but what he saw confused him even more. The tattoo was gone. "What? I could have sworn . . ." his voice trailed off, and then he looked at his fellow fishermen with righteous indignation. "I wasn't staring at them!"

An older sailor, sunburned and with hair the color of dirty

snow, winked at him. "No use getting yer britches in a bunch. She is quite a lovely, and she was naked as the day she was born!"

The other sailors hooted, nodded in agreement, chuckling and making lewd comments and gestures.

Cyrus rose to his feet, holding her as if she were a child, determined to leave the juvenile, perverted sailors behind to attend their duties. "I'm taking her to my cabin."

More looks.

"Seriously. I'm just gonna make sure she's okay. Honest."

With them laughing at his back, Cyrus made his way below deck, the woman's face pressed against his chest, her thick, wavy hair tickling his scruffy chin. He smelled the salt from the sea and something else. Sandalwood? An earthy smell. Pleasant and real. Ever so gently, he laid the enigmatic female on his cot and made sure she was tucked in comfortably. A fierce instinct to protect her took root in his being. It shocked him, though it also felt natural on some level. Cyrus would safeguard her. That was that.

****

"Hey, hey . . . it's alright."

She shook her head, her face buried in the pillow, frustrated beyond all belief. A hot, angry tear burned a track down her cheek. Why did nothing make sense? How could something as simple as knowing her own damn name be such an impossibility?

She lifted her head and let out a long, disheartened sigh. Fresh tears continued to flow. She needed to get out of there. Now! She sprang from the bed and almost fell, tangled in the sheets due to the stiffness in her limbs. Frustrated, she growled. Pinpricks of pain jabbed her as nerves flared back to life with the flow of blood. She staggered, head bowed, half on the bed, one foot on the floor. Rage and confusion battled for dominance. An intense throbbing pulsed a beat in her temples. Her stomach churned, and her vision blurred. Something else slithered just beneath the surface.

Movement.

"Miss—"

A hand brushed her shoulder. She struck out blindly. A grunt of shock and perhaps pain as her fist connected with flesh. Her sight cleared in time for her to see poor Cyrus on the other side of the room, groaning as he held his stomach. Mortified, she looked down at her trembling hands. Then, before she knew it, she was at his side, tentative and ashamed. "I'm so sorry. I didn't mean to hurt you. I just snapped."

Cyrus looked at her, his eyes slitted in pain, but managed a shaky smile. "Like I said, it's alright. Just trying to help. But please, don't punch me again."

She knew he meant it as a joke, but she took it to heart. It must have shown in her eyes.

He exhaled and sat up. "I'm joking. Well, not really. I mean, don't hit me again, but what I was trying to say is—"

She raised her hand, relieved and somewhat amused. "I understand. I didn't realize I had that much strength. There's so much I don't know." She stared at the floor.

He rose to his feet and coughed. "I won't pretend to know what's going to happen next. But you clearly need some help. And I," he held up his arms, indicating the small cabin, "could use a little direction myself. If I can help, why not?"

The woman tilted her head to the side like a cat. "Really? You would help me? You don't even know me."

A mischievous grin found its way onto his lips. "Hey, you don't even know yourself."

Despite herself, the woman who came from the sea found herself chuckling. Pressure lifted from her shoulders, replaced by hope. "Indeed."

****

That night, she dreamed of a great many thing. Images, vivid and cinematic, seemingly plucked from time like ripe fruit from a branch, suddenly remembered by her. But how? Such events were cold, dead, expressionless words without memory now printed on the dusty, withered face of textbooks found in schools and universities. Impossible recollections of historical events that no one was old enough to remember. Even the world's oldest person would have read the images in books now turned to dust and delegated to oral recitation. The touch, the taste, the smell of living history stamped permanently on time itself, forever bonded, flickered in her mind.

She stirred, exhaling softly, then lay on her side, the sheets entangling her limbs. She was dreaming of Africa—younger, newer, and teeming with life. Life in the veld had been paradise. Plentiful game. The young frolicked as mothers congregated, laughing and talking, one eye perpetually on their spirited young ones. The men were hunting, and the wizened elderly were rooted in the cool, sweet shade. There was no strife. A veritable Garden of Eden. Seemingly perfect.

Off to the side stood a figure who appeared much older than the wrinkly, toothless elders. Something about him seemed . . . out of place. A part of the people and yet apart. Beneath his heavy brow, pestered by flies, his hooded eyes, almost black, watched over them like a sentinel. She realized it even in her dream state and felt her body turn uncomfortably. The movement must have caught the strange man's eye. Ever so slowly, he turned toward her. She froze and then gasped as his eyes locked with hers.

She forced herself awake.

"What?" her voice sounded like sandpaper. She looked down at her arms, which were covered in goose bumps. A chill swept through her body. Suddenly, the room felt hot. The burning image of the mysterious man's face lingered. Chalky ash paint over black, withered skin. Tall, his neck adorned in golden rings. Cracked white flakes floated from his still form. His dried lips were half-parted, a frozen sentence upon them. Intent eyes bore into her soul. She felt nauseous and shaky. She needed air.

She stumbled out onto the deck, where a cluster of fishermen were talking. One glanced at her, and the talking stopped. She spotted Cyrus and ignored the fishermen as she made her way to him, her stomach complaining.

One look at her face darkened his features. "What's wrong?" He stepped back from the rail on which he had been leaning, no longer lost in thought. Wherever his mind had been, now it was planted firmly in the present.

She joined him at the rail. They were preparing to dock. Fear fluttered in her stomach. Her next step was daunting. She had not expected to remain on the boat forever, coddled within its bubble of safety, and yet, leaving its confines made her more than a little nervous. Scared. "I'm sorry to burden you with this. I can understand if you want us to go our separate ways once we're ashore."

Cyrus arched his eyebrow and gave her a sideways glance. "Are you serious? You're joking, right?"

She looked up at him, confused. "Haven't I caused enough trouble?"

Her tall rescuer chuckled and slowly shook his head. "Lady, you almost *drowned*. What you need is some food in your stomach and a doctor to make sure you're alright."

She continued to look at him, relief and gratitude grappling with her ever-present fear. She let out a soft sigh and then tucked a wavy lock of hair behind her ear. Her gaze soaked in the bay's dark beauty. It had nearly claimed her life and stolen her memories in the process. Almost drowned? She recalled Cyrus's words. No, it seemed more permanent, more final. There was so much she did not know. And now with the dream seeming so real, so tangible, and that old man . . . so much was not adding up. Answers were necessary. From all. Curiosity nagged at her. It was imperative she know more about this mystery man who had saved her life.

"So, this is all from the kindness of your heart?" There was no other way to say it. Better to be upfront instead of tiptoeing around. "I don't mean to sound ungrateful. Believe me, I'm not. I just want to put it out there that I have no money or anything. I don't want you to—"

"Don't."

"I just mean—"

"Really. Don't."

"I—"

"Seriously. Don't insult me. I'm aware of the fact that you were full out naked without a shred of clothing. Where would you hide money?"

She blushed.

Cyrus realized what he had said a second too late. "Sorry. That didn't come out right. Change of topic. You came out here looking worried. Is something else bothering you?"

She exhaled, thoughts returning to the dream like water circling around a drain, down, down, down to who knew where. A moist, spiraling darkness deep in the earth. A darkness where her memories, her past life, was sequestered. She realized her hands were knotted into fists. As if to accentuate her frustration, her stomach let out an embarrassing growl.

Cyrus looked at her and at her stomach and then returned his gaze to her face. She knew he saw worry in her startling blue eyes. It seemed to make a home there. Her body vibrated with tension, embarrassment almost overshadowing her distress. She could not meet his gaze. Absently, she pressed her stomach.

"Yeah . . . I know a place where we can eat."

****

O'Malley's was less than ten minutes from Trinity Inlet, where *Peaches* was docked. She was grateful the commute was fast. However, it was not fast enough to prevent a few more gastronomical rumblings in the backseat of the cab. Cyrus and the cab driver were respectfully quiet. No one wanted to risk the dark-skinned woman's smoldering glare.

O'Malley's was an Irish bar, Cyrus's favorite spot. Bewilderment knotted her brow, as she had been expecting a restaurant, but then the dimly lit atmosphere pulled her in. Hunger was a raging beast rattling the cage of her stomach. Cyrus put his hand on her shoulder as he directed her toward a table in the back. Relief squeezed a soft sigh from her lips once she sat down.

"Thank you," she said, as if on autopilot.

"Yeah, no problem," Cyrus replied, looking for a waiter or waitress. He did not have to wait long. A young man wearing a black T-shirt with the restaurant's logo on it sauntered over holding two glasses of water. He placed the glasses before them, not quite looking at them yet. A notepad peeked out from a pocket in his apron. A pen was inserted between his left ear and temple. When the young man looked up, he looked at her and then Cyrus but then returned his gaze to the woman, staring at her a little too long for her liking.

Discomfort warmed her from within. She knew what he must be thinking. Here was a girl wearing baggy clothes, obviously, men's clothes, looking rough, and out with a guy who looked just as scruffy. Vagabonds? Unfit for the establishment? Or maybe it was their dark complexion? The woman bristled. Unbeknownst to her, the water in her glass began to bubble.

"Are you going to take my order or continue staring?"

"Ma'am, I—" The waiter flushed with a sudden wave of embarrassment.

"Sorry," Cyrus said, hand raised to diffuse the tense situation. "It's been a long day. Very long."

Still embarrassed, the server nodded quickly, eyes averted. "Yes, sir. I was just going to say I liked her shirt. I can . . . I can come back when you're ready."

Just as suddenly as her anger had built, guilt dampened her ardor, followed by regret. She looked up and read his name tag: "Jeremy." Had she been projecting her own insecurities and feelings regarding their Salvation Army-esque attire? Perhaps. "Forgive me. It's like he said. It's been a long day. It's not every day you come back from the dead."

"Ma'am?" Jeremy raised an eyebrow.

"More time, please?" Cyrus pleaded; two fingers pinched on the bridge of his nose.

Jeremy was gone before Cyrus could blink. Cyrus rolled his eyes toward the mystery woman. "So, are you going to snap at everyone? Or are you just that hungry?"

Pinpricks of irritation settled uneasily over her. She pursed her lips, chewed on the inside of her cheek, and avoided his eyes. She took in the framed pictures of all shapes and sizes mounted on the mint-colored wall. Newspaper clippings and ads, current and much, much older. The vintage clock. The worn wooden finish. The "O'Malley's" sign on the wall, glowing faintly. The hushed chatter and the occasional outburst of laughter. Maybe they were not looking at her. Maybe they were not grilling them.

Paranoia. Ugh. She raked her hand through her mass of tumbling curls. *Take a deep breath, get it together,* she coached herself. She felt warm, so she rolled up her sleeves and rested her elbows on the table, hands clasped, chin resting on top. Darkness blurred her vision, and she closed her eyes, shielding them from reality. Her leg began to shake.

"Hello?"

She looked up, momentarily confused, then focused on Cyrus's concerned face. "Yes?"

"Never mind," he muttered as Jeremy returned.

Once they had placed their orders and were alone again, she took a long sip of water. No sign of the bubbles. Placid and untouched. Still, no one had noticed. Not even her. She watched his Adam's apple bob up and down as he drank, transfixed, lost in thought. He let out a satisfied "ahhhh" after he drank from his own glass and then noticed her looking. She yanked her eyes away. He smirked.

The meaning of his question finally sank in. Embarrassment reared its ugly head once again. "I'm sorry. Just distracted. I didn't mean to snap."

Her knight in grungy denim shrugged casually. All mock modesty. "It's cool. I was just making sure I knew how to get along with you, uh . . . I think we're going to need to pick a name for you. At least until you remember your real name. Is that okay?"

The mysterious woman smiled, curious. "Are you for real?"

Again with the shrug. "I can't keep on saying 'you' or, to myself, 'that woman' or 'her,' right?"

She laughed despite herself. "Right!"

Cyrus rubbed his hands together, the prospect of a game adding some excitement to what had been a tense situation. "So, let's see here . . . How about Debra?"

She shook her head.

"Ann?"

She raised her eyebrow.

His hands went up as if to forestall any more denial. "No and no, gotcha. How about something a little more contemporary?

Maybe something cutesy like Toni?"

She sipped her water again, grinning, then shook her head. "They're all very nice names, but they don't do it for me."

Grinning, Cyrus slumped back in his chair, his green eyes twinkling. "They're not good enough for ya?"

Smirk still in place, she shrugged. "They just aren't me. They don't sum me up."

"Still playing that mystery card?"

She did not answer right away. "This isn't a game. I'm just something else, I guess."

At that point, Jeremy returned with their food. The woman's stomach welcomed him audibly. Being famished beyond belief left no room or time for talking. Her body had endured a lot in the past few hours, and sustenance was mandatory. As she dug in, the glass of water before her showed no signs of unusual activity.

5

"Paperwork? I hate paperwork."

In truth, they should have gone to the hospital first, but she had been too hungry. It was possible they would have fed her at the hospital, but why take the chance? Cyrus was learning quickly that he did not want to keep *her* from a plate of food. So, a quick detour had been more than necessary.

The hospital in question, Cairns Hospital, was only four or five minutes from the bar. With full bellies, the odd pair went to get her checked out to be sure there were no lingering effects from her time in the water.

Cyrus stood at the reception desk in the vast, empty waiting room looking over the documents they were required to sign. However, there was a problem. A big one. He could not answer a simple question like the patient's name. Even she did not know.

He swept a hand through his dark hair and turned to her. She was standing off to the side, oblivious. She seemed so out of place in the waiting room's harsh lights. Skittish and nervous. A mop of dark curls framed her face but could not hide the uncertainty in her strangely colored blue eyes. Dressed in his clothes, she stood out rather than blended in. What was her story? People did not just end up in the middle of the ocean! Cyrus was stumped. Confused. Frustrated. Intrigued.

She approached him. He nodded at the forms. "Paperwork."

She leaned in close and narrowed her eyes at the print on the white sheets of paper. She shifted her focus to his pen. Slowly, she reached for it. "Such a strange writing utensil. From fingers dipped in mud to quills dipped in inkwells to . . . a pen? A pen, yes, filled with ink. How odd." A faraway look floated into her blue eyes. "I have no name to put down."

Cyrus exhaled, frustration within arm's reach. "Yeah, I know. It makes filling this out even more difficult. We haven't even gotten to your medical history, insurance, and what have you. Maybe we should have gone to a clinic."

She tilted her head to the side, wistful. A curl escaped and spilled across her cheek. "I suspect they would have required the basics too. I wish I remembered."

A bored nurse dressed in soft pastel colors glanced toward them. Suspicion lifted an eyebrow. The nurse wore no makeup. Squat with not even a hint of curvature, she shuffled over and glanced at the packet of documents, which were still oddly devoid of any personal information. She looked back and forth between Cyrus and the woman. "Is there a problem?"

Before she could answer, Cyrus cut in, afraid of what embarrassing thing she would say. "Honestly, Nurse . . ." His eyes rolled toward her name tag. "Becky, yes, there is. This woman has just suffered severe trauma. She nearly drowned not too far from Trinity Inlet. My crew and I were shrimping, and we found her floating in the water. She doesn't remember her name or anything else that might be helpful. So, here we are." He finally took a breath.

Nurse Becky's face shifted instantly from distrust to worry and empathy. "Oh my. I'm so sorry. Did you file a police report?"

The thought had not crossed their minds. As one, they shook their heads. Nurse Becky shook her head in reprimand and then leaned in close. Her breath smelled of coffee and cigarettes. The chewing gum was doing a poor job of disguising both.

"Just give these to me," she whispered, looking from side to side, then snatching the paperwork. Cyrus suppressed a grin. "It's slow tonight," she said. "Thank God. Why don't you have a seat over there? I'll find a room for you. A doctor will be with you shortly."

Nurse Becky seemed awfully pleased with herself, and rightfully so. She had done her good deed for the day. The patient and her handsome friend looked like two fish out of water. If she could help them, she would. Cyrus and the woman were relieved.

****

Much to the hospital's credit, the doctor, Dr. Winslow, was thorough and had an enviable bedside manner. As Cyrus waited outside, she felt safe with the doctor. He asked basic questions, and she answered as best as she could. He redressed the cuts and scrapes marking her body. Blood and urine samples were sent off to be tested. As they were wrapping up, he jotted down the last of his notes while leaning against the wall. She was seated in a hospital gown with her hands on her lap awaiting his prognosis.

"Thank you, Dr. Winslow," she replied politely, weary beyond belief. "I'm glad there are no life-threatening injuries."

He nodded. "If you wish, you can rest here for a few hours. I'll check in on you in a few hours. Please rest."

"Of course, doctor," she replied, her mind already reeling with the possibilities of her next step. Cyrus filled her thoughts. The thought of him oddly eased the knot of tension in her stomach. The man with the green eyes *had* been there every step of the way. "I just need a few hours of sleep, and then I'll be on my way."

Dr. Winslow pushed off the wall and reached out to shake her hand. "No rush. You just rest. We'll keep you for observation, just in case."

As soon as he was gone, she slumped onto the bed and let sleep claim her. In less than five minutes, she drifted off.

****

Sometime during the (what seemed to be) long, uneventful night, a nurse hooked up an IV bag to hydrate the mysterious woman and checked her vitals. A glass of water was on the nightstand by her bed. Cyrus hovered as the nurse attended to the woman he had known for only a few hours but for whom he felt responsible. Once they were alone, he scooted his chair close to her head, plopped down, rose again when he noticed an abandoned newspaper, picked it up, and sat back down. He skimmed the paper for several minutes before getting up to go get a cup of coffee.

****

The hiss of the hospital equipment joined the sound of her soft breathing. The room was dimly lit. The half-empty glass of water was still on her nightstand. Her explosion of curls were spread across the pillow, her forehead creased with worry. A troubled sleep to be sure. No surprise there. The half-opened newspaper remained in the chair beside her bed. Cyrus had not returned yet.

Another visitor entered the room. A nurse, a different one from earlier. She entered on silent nursing clogs. She was immersed in shadow as she made her way to the patient's bed, a syringe in hand. The young woman was lying with her back to her. Slowly, the nurse reached for her shoulder and turned her over so she could see her clearly. Yes, it was *her*. Better to end things quickly. She began to administer the toxin into the IV bag.

"Hello?"

She hissed and then spun around to behold a tall, broad-shouldered man of Middle Eastern descent dumbly returning her gaze. He was holding a cup of coffee and a bag of peanut M&Ms. Their eyes locked.

He could not stop thinking about her. He barely registered paying for the coffee and M&Ms. What was the next course of action? What was his next move? What was their next move? So caught up in his thoughts, Cyrus hardly noticed opening the bedroom door where his strange friend slept. Frozen in his tracks, his mind refused to process what his eyes were witnessing. A strange woman hovering over his sleeping friend. "Hello?"

Cyrus saw that her eyes were black, without pupils. Inky tears streamed down cheeks that looked more withered and drained by the second.

"Holy sh—"

A wail, a shriek that held all the fury, all the rage, all the hate of this world burst from the nurse's cracked, blackened lips as she charged Cyrus.

Fear and shock overwhelmed him, rooted him to the spot of his guaranteed death. In that moment, he saw the nurse's perfectly coiffed hair transform into streamers of what appeared to be dirty straw, long and filthy. Her mouth opened to reveal a maw full of wet blackness and a thrashing black tongue that reminded him of a snake rolling in wet dirt. Her ear-splitting, soul-rending shriek was going to split him in two.

She moved in; syringe raised as a weapon.

Cyrus looked down at his coffee and then threw it in her face.

The nurse—who was clearly not really a nurse—screamed even louder, which did not seem possible. Momentarily blinded, she struck out with her clawed hand and shoved Cyrus to the side. He cried out in pain as he skidded into a wall. Her claws had cut through his sleeve and left bloody cuts across his right arm. The monster in nursing clogs spun around, still temporarily blinded, and lashed out at him again. Cursing, he brought up his uninjured arm to defend himself as he attempted to kick the creature. She caught his foot and lifted him off the floor.

"Little bag o' meat and bones," it whispered, its foul breath smelling of death. Its tears reminded him of seawater and tar. "Did ye think ye can stop a woman o' the barrows?"

Blood rushed to his head as she dangled him upside down. His head pounded, and yet he still tried to muster up some bravado. "Lady, c-c-could you reach into my pocket?"

The wailing woman raised a crusty eyebrow. "What?"

"T-t-there's a pack of gum . . . p-p-probably not enough for you though."

She let out another ear-piercing howl that caused his ears to bleed as she tossed him aside. He hit another wall; the air crushed out of his lungs. Stars exploded in his vision. Nausea rolled uneasily and sent questing fingers out from his stomach. Something warm and hot trickled down his forehead and over his right eye. *Great. Just freakin' great*, Cyrus thought, stitches of pain all over his body. He blinked away blood just in time to see the creature glide over to the mysterious woman in the bed.

"Oh, no you don't!" he sputtered, rising despite the pain and barreling into the supernatural creature. They rolled around in a knot of limbs, blocked hits, and sliced arms. As long as there was breath in his body, he would make sure she was safe. There would be no harm brought to her. But judging by what he was up against, breath would not remain in his body for long.

Still, he fought, but he knew it was in vain.

The monster was too powerful.

"Do ye have any last words?" the creature hissed as she throttled Cyrus. Much to his horror, he felt his strength ebb. Blood poured from his forehead as he heard alarmed shouts outside the room. No doubt the staff were trying to see what was going on, but the overturned dresser had blocked the door.

A headache pounded behind the cut above his eye. The agonizing pain swept through his body in shuddering waves. The witch squeezed the air from his lungs as she tightened her grip. He tried to answer, but words failed him. His eyelids got heavier, and his flailing limbs lost strength. Darkness ate at the fringes of his vision. Then something caught his eye. Something remarkable. A mischievous grin pulled at his bloodied lips. "Yeah . . . I do. Look behind you."

The creature wearing the dead flesh of an old woman turned around and then hissed in shock. Floating above the bed was the woman with no name. Her dark curls blew in an unnatural wind, and her azure eyes glowed. One hand was raised, as if to pronounce judgment. She had a terrible beauty to her. Her eyes were narrowed with fury, and her full lips were pursed tight. Her feet barely touched the bed's surface. Her unique tattoo reappeared and burned like a smoldering brand on her breast. The fluids inside the IV bag bubbled as if they were on a stove.

"Release him, banshee, and do it now."

The banshee's black tears continued to fall. For a moment, she faltered and cursed in a language not in uttered in centuries. Was that fear in her eyes? Whatever it was, it quickly dissolved and drifted down her alabaster cheeks. "No, lass. Ye must die. It has been commanded."

The levitating woman in the hospital gown narrowed her eyes into slits of chilling fury. "By whom?"

"The emissary!" the banshee bellowed as she recommenced her original mission—the execution of her.

It happened so fast. The mysterious woman raised her hand higher and called out to the watery contents of the IV bag. A moment later, the solution burst free and coiled around her raised hands. It swirled faster and faster, fluid rings a whirling blur. Her eyes never stopped glowing as she grunted and redirected the solution directly into the banshee's face. The banshee choked and sputtered and tried in vain to block the water.

It's not enough, she whispered internally, calling for more assistance from a part of her that she had no idea existed. Still, that spark, that nucleus allowed her to continue to do the impossible. The pipes under the sink in the adjacent bathroom burst and let loose a geyser of water under her control. It snaked toward the banshee. Sweat gathered on the mysterious woman's brow and upper lip as she continued her aquatic assault on the creature that meant to kill her and Cyrus. It was taxing, as evidence by her dropping to one knee, one hand still raised.

Come on . . . you can do this! she screamed internally. *I'm not sure how this is possible, but I . . . I trust it. I must trust in it, as I trust Cyrus!* This refueled her efforts and made the nimbus of her calling even more advantageous. What felt like cool rejuvenating ice water thrummed within. Every inch of her body, every cell screamed for this mysterious, newfound ability. It sang of its glory, its immense power. In short, she craved it. Craved the promise of power, the complete control she so desperately needed at that juncture in her brief life. Plus, he needed her.

"The emissary?" she asked, her question squeezed out in a strained hiss. She rose to her full height, and her muscles trembled. Nerves of flame turned to ice; eyes lost to a blaze of cerulean power. She knotted her fists at her sides and then raised them over her head. The show of force manifested in a geyser of water that sent the banshee into the air, drowning and kicking. The stream of water held her in place, encircled her waist, as the empowered attacker willed it. She glided over until she and the banshee were just inches apart.

The banshee sobbed, its face twisted in grief and rage. "Yes . . . yes . . . he be the one who ordered ye death!"

For a moment, she was caught off-guard. "An assassination attempt? Why?"

The wailing creature responded with a head butt. Pain exploded in the woman's sight, and her grip on the animated water diminished. Gravity reclaimed the airborne amnesiac and gracelessly dumped her on all fours. Pain shot hot daggers into her upon impact, stinging her palms and sending jolts through her kneecaps to the rest of her body. A nursing clog struck her under the chin and snapped her head back. The momentum sent her into the wall. A small crater formed from the impact as she slid down. The banshee turned its hungry gaze back to Cyrus, who was struggling to his feet, and lunged for him.

"No!"

Time seemed to slow as the nameless woman who had risen from the depths of the ocean screamed for more of the elixir to sustain life. She summoned it from every water pipe inside the hospital. Pure, unbridled power flowed through her as she ordered the constant flow of dam-bursting water directly at the banshee. The full power of the attack sent the banshee through the window into the night air, screeching the entire way.

With a flick of her wrists, she halted the trajectory of the jettisoned banshee, who was shackled once more by the liquid restraints, held in place high above the street below. The woman flexed her fists once more. The water shackles tightened, drawing her closer to the creature, both suspended in the air outside the hospital. Not far from their current airborne position, she heard the lapping of waves on the shore. Only she heard it from within. An invisible thread connected them. Her next choice was clear.

"You were warned not to lay a hand on my friend. Tell your master he does not intimidate me."

Despite her predicament, the withered creature with black tears and even blacker teeth sneered. "You have manifested. He already knows. The serpent will come. He will—"

The next threat gurgled in her throat as bubbling black blood rose from the creature's dead insides. The woman gasped as the banshee choked to death on her own blood. Was she doing this? She was not sure. She was not sure of anything. They made eye contact, and in that moment, she saw true fear in the banshee's eyes. The creature whispered something and then exploded in chunks of blackened flesh and blood. Being in the direct vicinity of the explosion, the woman's face and body were sprayed with it. It smelled of decaying flesh and brine.

Gagging, she covered her mouth with a filthy hand and flew back into the room through the shattered window.

Cyrus, poor bloody Cyrus, was braced against the wall holding his torn arm, obviously in pain. Her heart went out to him as she approached, concern making her eyes bright.

Cyrus squinted at her, probably trying to reconcile the woman in the bed with the woman before him, who was covered in sooty, fleshy bits, her feet barely touching the ground. It was too much to take in.

"Are you okay?" she asked, gingerly putting a hand on his shoulder.

He winced but did not turn when her hand rested on him. "That's the second-most-asked question I keep asking you," he stammered, gritting his teeth against the pain.

"Is it? And what's the first?" she replied coyly, aware of where this was going.

A smirk tried and then failed to crease his pained face. "Who in the hell are you?"

In truth, she still had no answer for him. That did not deter her from seeking the truth in a world growing more uncertain by the minute.

"Still trying to figure that out, Cyrus. I know now that I'm important enough to be killed."

"By a monster wearing orthopedic shoes," he quipped. Gingerly, he stepped away from the wall and forced his green eyes to focus on her glowing orbs, the power within them dimming slowly. "Can't say I'm surprised. There was quite a storm when I saved you. Naked."

She lifted her eyebrow. "We're back to me being naked?"

"Maybe," Cyrus teased. "But first we gotta get patched up and—"

Before he could finish his statement, the door flew open, sending the dresser airborne. Three orderlies and two security guards followed by two nurses crammed into the room. There was a moment of silence, and then the room erupted in chaos.

6

She had barely taken in her surroundings when she and Cyrus were shoved through the doors of the busy Cairns police station. Her head was bowed, but she soaked in her surroundings just the same. Despite the pounding headache and the sudden depletion in strength, she could smell the coffee, hear the expressive shouts of officers, and determine just how cramped and confined it was. In her peripheral vision, she saw drunkards handcuffed to benches sleeping off their stupor.

Cyrus remained silent, head also bowed. He shuffled along, stiffer than usual, but when one had cuts and bruised ribs, that was to be expected. Once hospital security had entered the room and determined Cyrus and the woman were no threat, they were both evaluated. Cyrus showed no signs of a concussion, which is why they had been whisked away immediately for questioning. No one could understand why he was beat up, and she . . . well, she was covered in something black, wet, and putrid. They forced her to shower before they left the hospital.

Once again, she wore hand-me-down clothing, courtesy of former patients, alive or dead, as did Cyrus. Her hair was still wet from her quick shower. They spoke not a word until they were taken in separate directions.

"Cyrus?"

His head snapped up, worry evident in the green pools of his eyes. He tried to walk toward her, but two plainclothes police officers blocked his path. He winced in pain from the many wounds blemishing his body. "It's alright. You'll be fine. Just hang in there."

She knew he meant to be reassuring, but uncertainty gnawed at her. The recent battle with the banshee (how had she known that name?) and the sudden manifestation of her own powers raised more questions than answers. Something nagged at the back of her mind. Almost a memory...

Her eyebrows were bunched in confusion as the police officers led her into an interrogation room. Dim lighting. Cramped with just enough room for a desk with two chairs. A video camera was present, but no green light indicated it was on. She observed all this from behind the curtain of locks that covered her eyes.

Two officers were present. One was a tall, lanky woman with ash-blond hair pulled back severely into a ponytail. She was showing the signs of middle age, but she had probably been pretty when she was younger. Time on the force had hollowed out her cheeks and added deep crow's feet around her eyes. She wore a buttoned-up blazer over a button-down shirt. Her name tag read "Detective Regan."

The other officer was her opposite in every way. He was shorter by a few inches, but what he lacked in height he made up for it in width. The fabric of his shirt was stretched, the buttons in silent protest. A five o' clock shadow peppered with white covered his jowls. His eyes appeared sunken. A permanent sneer was printed on his face. His name tag read "Sergeant Avis."

"G'day, ma'am," Detective Regan began. "We don't seem to have a name for you. But before we begin, can I get you something? Coffee? Maybe water?"

Water.

That was the trigger.

She raised her head but did not see them anymore. Nor did she see the interrogation room or the video camera recording her. She did not hear Detective Regan slip further into her "good cop" routine. The flickering light. The press of bodies. They blurred as a sound became more prevalent. It sounded like the dripping of water. Slow and rhythmic. Echoes. Perhaps in a hollow place? Memory, ever elusive and unpredictable, took her back to an hour before . . .

A cave protected her from the oppressive heat outside. It was cool and dark and seemed to stretch on forever. She found herself a few feet inside the cave entrance, the sun's warmth still on her back. Only a moment before, she had fallen asleep. Right? Was this not a dream? She stepped farther into the cavern, lured by the sound of plopping water. She paused and looked back, afraid. Would she return to the blissful heat of the African sun, or would she tread deeper into the cavern? Something called to her. She took another step into the cavern.

It was bigger inside. A somewhat dizzying illusion. Stalactites protruded like dew-tipped daggers from the ceiling. Gingerly, she meandered around rocks and stalagmites upon the ground. The soothing coolness seeped into the soles of her bare feet. She looked down and noticed she was wearing a hospital gown. What was going on? What was happening? A siren call spoke to her core. All she could do was go deeper.

Cave drawings got her attention. Stick figures in lurid colors illustrating a story. A female in the middle surrounded by her peers. They were black. To the side was another figure—taller with white markings over his black stick figure. An entwined stylized bird and Egyptian-looking symbol enclosed them all. She stopped to observe the image. Tentatively, her fingers hovered over the etched drawings. An odd sensation settled over her the closer she got to the wall. Magic buzzed and pulsed from the slightly shimmering figures, and if she looked close enough, movement. Perhaps it was clearer in her peripheral vision because when she walked past it, the figures came to life—the males swaying around the female. The woman was glowing. Aquamarine dye pulsed on the craggy wall.

The cavern grew cooler, the dripping sounds louder. Not far in the distance, a light glowed. "Curiouser and curiouser," she recited from *Alice in Wonderland*. And there was another sliver of trivia, information she had no idea about. What was going on in her head? Selective amnesia? Thoughts buzzed in her mind as she came upon a small open area. A small fire blazed and crackled. A pool of rejuvenating water was a few feet away. And there sat a tall, wizened man with his legs crossed. The dancing flames cast eerie shadows on the cracked white powder that dusted his pitch-black skin. She froze.

The man from her dream!

The one eye she could see appeared completely black in the flickering light given off by the flames. Boredom emanated from him. Claw scars, echoes of an old battle, were stamped across his face. One scar bisected one of his eyes, leaving it a milky, sightless orb. He continued to stare.

The woman, who seemed less of a mystery in present company, took a furtive step closer. "I . . . I remember you. Can you tell me what's going on?"

He did not respond. Instead, he stirred the fire with a stick. After a long moment, his eyes rolled up to ensnare her own with grave intensity. "What is going on is that you are late. Or perhaps you are on time?" His voice sounded ancient. His eyes seemed older still. And yet, confusion fluttered across those sunken orbs like wispy clouds across a midnight sky. Ironically, resolution and haughty indignation filled the void. "I have been waiting a long, long time for you, my child."

"Your child? Are you saying I'm your daughter?" Warring emotions inflamed her. Chief among them were shock, confusion, and hope.

The old man unfolded his long limbs and rose slowly to his full height. He shook his head. "My issue? No, it was never meant that way. And yet, you are all my children. But you haven't much time."

Before she knew it, she had closed the distance between them, questions bursting on the tip of the tongue. "What? I don't understand. Who am I? Where am I? Who are yo—"

He shook his bony, withered head, his dusty dreadlocks swaying with the movement. "Girl, you are asking the wrong questions. You time-slipped during your dream. It brought you here. You are in grave danger. And so is the fisherman."

Fear flowed through her veins like ice water. Confusion, a sensation with which she was becoming annoyingly familiar, mired her features once again. The fisherman? She had to remember. There was another. An ally. What was his name? Why was it so hard to remember? The cave seemed to grow mistier. The glow of the fire and the lapping of water lulled her. "I can barely recall—"

"You don't remember because this memory is altered by the flow of time," he replied thickly, ushering her toward the water. "I marked this cave as a beacon, a time-slip for you. I foresaw it countless ages ago—the possibility, anyway. You recall it now because it is how you remember. But now with the recent break and the arrival of the fisherman—"

"Cyrus!"

There it was! Cyrus was her friend *and* the fisherman. She recalled his captivating eyes, which reminded her of the blush of new spring. Unshed tears swam in her vision. He was in the now, the present, but she was not. She was somewhere no more substantial than a fever dream. The old man's warning seemed real though.

"My friend's name is Cyrus. He was checking on me at the hospital. Is he..."

Her voice trailed off as the elderly man with dark skin covered in powder knelt before the water and gestured for her to do the same. "Alive for now. Now be silent. *Listen*. The wheel is broken. Darkness is a web that connects your brave new world. Beware. A messenger of death is outside your door. You cannot protect your ears from the wailing of a banshee. Now look."

Kneeling, she looked at him and then to where he gestured, which was the pool of water. Her reflection stared back at her. Then, for a moment, she saw something unexpected. Golden, multicolored rings adorned her throat, and her upper torso was swathed in a form-fitting, off-the-shoulder garment. Her unruly mane of curls cascaded past her shoulders. Hoop earrings glittered in the reflection. Colorful tribal paint artfully streaked her face. A blue dot had been painted on her forehead. Her lips were luscious, black, and glistening.

She blinked.

Her eyes opened to behold her plain, unassuming hospital gown. What was going on? She rubbed the creases in her forehead. The experience added yet another layer of unexplainable confusion since her hectic return from the dead.

"What did you see?" the old man inquired as his fingers trailed in the water. His voice had a knowing tone.

She shook her head. A headache began to awaken. "Something impossible. Something I can't explain. Like so many things in my life."

"So, just because you cannot explain it, it is impossible?" he countered, a rueful twinkle in his eyes as he continued to stir the waters. "Look again."

For some strange reason, she obeyed. There was a mystifying element to this man; cagey and elusive yet seeming to emanate secret knowledge. In fact, she detected a sense of deep-rooted forlornness, an aching loneliness behind his cryptic words, his insistent commands. As if he were the consummate outcast, on the outside looking in. Something she had been familiar with since she opened her eyes. A familiarity connected the two.

The hairs on her neck and forearms stood up. Then déjà vu rolled over in her a skin-tingling wave. Had she experienced this moment before? She returned her gaze to her reflection. A different woman stared back. She blinked again. Now another woman beheld her. After a few more times of this dizzying kaleidoscope of different faces, different walks of life, the surface rippled, and the images wavered. Suddenly angry, she stood up and dusted off her knees. "Why can't you just tell me who I am?" Tears of frustration stung her eyes, and her bottom lip trembled.

The old man also stood up, long limbs popping and cracking, a solemn look on his face. Slowly, he raised his hand and cupped her chin. His callous skin was rough. "I cannot tell you who you are, my little sparrow. That grand question must be answered by you and you alone. We are joined by others on our journey through life, but at some point, we must walk alone. Self-identity is a crucial internal process. No one can tell us who we are. You must choose. You must decide."

She yanked away from him. "Then why are we here? Why did you summon me here? You said my friend was in danger!"

As if in answer, the cave shook. Dust drifted down from the

ceiling. The water rippled. Alarm widened her eyes. She grabbed his arm. "Send me back! I have to help Cyrus."

The old man looked down at her. "I just needed you to know that you have great power. You need to discover who you are if you hope to stop the tidal wave of darkness that is about to wash over you."

Fear warmed her insides, and the desperation to return to Cyrus infused her with a burst of adrenaline. The cave shook again. For a moment, her surroundings flickered like the disturbed water. She felt even more disconnected from her vicinity. "Okay, please wake me up."

The old man nodded and held her hand. "The realms are blending now. Reconcile who you were with who you will be. Therein lies your gift. Now wake up, and silence the *bean sith*, the banshee." He pressed a fingertip to her forehead and whispered in a voice like wind turning pages and the dry heat of the plains, "Find the scribe. Try to remember. Now awaken."

Darkness, her oldest friend, covered her like a welcoming blanket, rushed over her like a waterfall. She did not fight it. She surrendered to the constant flow, which carried her way from the cave locked in time, rooted in her memory, and let it sweep her into the sterile present of reality. Her eyes had opened just in time to see the banshee about to claim Cyrus's life. She did not remember rising from the bed, but she did recall feeling a sweet pressure building in every cell of her body. She remembered hearing the stream of water, but not with her ears. With her soul. And her soul had told her to save the fisherman. "Release him, banshee. And do it now."

Water.

The dripping of water.

A cup placed before the blinking woman, the memory, the revelation now laid before her, wet and glistening.

"Ma'am?"

She blinked and tried to focus on the officers, who were staring at her quizzically. The scowl on Sergeant Avis's face deepened. He radiated suspicion, but she did not care.

"Yes . . . yes, I'm sorry. It's just been a very brutal day."

Detective Regan nodded sympathetically. "I can only imagine. We have many questions to ask you. But when you zone out, well, it makes it hard for us to continue."

The nameless woman nodded. "It was not my intention." A dream half-remembered nagged at her. The fisherman? A scribe? Fragments of a dream? The nagging doubts and pieces of memory felt akin to pinpricks of blood flowing through the nerves of recently awakened limbs that had fallen asleep

"Well, Miss," Detective Regan replied. "Get comfortable. We're going to go through the missing persons' reports, and then we're going to find out what just happened at the hospital. Then there's the matter of property damage."

She knew she could not stay there. A sense of foreboding imprinted on her mind, branded on her heart, created a sour aftertaste in her mouth. *Darkness is a web that connects your brave new world*. Dark words portended a bleak future. She had to find a way to get out of there.

And find the scribe.

****

The view was panoramic. Glittering lights of a city skyline. At first glance, it could have been any city. Its inhabitants carried on, immersed in the tasks before them—shopping, driving, preparing dinner, making love. They were naught but ants. Unsuspecting. Oblivious. All under his watchful gaze.

The well-dressed businessman stood against the floor-length window. The lights were off. His laptop's screensaver had been on for the better part of an hour. The office was spacious and spartan in its decor. Monochromatic. Sleek. Efficient.

His hands were pressed together, fingertips under his clean-shaven chin when a rectangle of light signified the entrance of another.

"Sir?"

He turned around as his personal aide stepped in holding a sheaf of documents. Black-rimmed glasses sat on his baby face. "Sir," he repeated, "you gave me explicit orders regarding the vessel."

A predatory smile tugged at the corner of the shadow-enshrouded man's mouth. "Indeed, Emmanuel?"

Emmanuel approached the desk and laid the documents on it, then used his index finger to push his glasses up the bridge of his nose. "Yes, indeed, sir. The vessel manifested in Cairns, Australia. The sisters alerted me. So, accordingly, I made the necessary arrangements to dispatch one of the agents to stop her. A banshee on retainer took the assignment. She was sent to the hospital." He paused, an uncomfortable look passing over his seemingly adolescent face.

The businessman stiffened. "And?"

Emmanuel cleared his throat and loosened his tie. "There were, uh, complications."

"Of course." The businessman sighed. "I'm puzzled though. The banshee could not stop a weakened woman?" He had to remind himself this was not just any woman. This was *her*. She needed to be dealt with at any cost.

"No, sir. The banshee was interrupted before she could kill the vessel."

The businessman arched his eyebrow. "Interrupted by what? Whom?"

"A man, sir."

"Just a man?"

"Yes, sir. I mean, no, sir."

"Explain."

"It was Cyrus."

"Cyrus?"

"Yes, sir. Cyrus Dhandi."

Silence. Then a roar of gut-wrenching laughter. Emmanuel shifted uneasily and averted his gaze.

"A small world indeed. Where are they now?"

Emmanuel pulled out his tablet, tapped it, and then looked up. "At the Cairns police station, sir."

A grin split the businessman's face. "Ah, yes. Two birds with one stone." He narrowed his eyes. "Is the situation under control?"

"Yes, sir. We already have our agents on the scene."

"Excellent. I've changed my mind. I want them both alive."

"Yes, sir."

7

Earlier

They were called the Sisters in the Deep Dark. They had always been referred to as such. Seven sisters shackled together in the dark with glowing eyes that reflected the light like the slitted pupils of a cat. The youngest was old enough for grade school. The oldest could have been in graduate school. They all had bone-bleached skin, a whiter shade of pale, and pale eyes sensitive to light, but they could see into the deep well of time, things yet to come. Their gifts were vast and far reaching. They should have been used for the betterment of the world.

Alas, they were not.

Their room was secreted in the bowels of the complex. Cool shadows and soothing darkness were all they knew. Well, that is not entirely true. They also knew what people were thinking, what they had eaten for breakfast, and what terrible sins darkened their hearts. The room was full of their whispers and chants, some throaty, some wispy, their voices in contrast, different pairs of eyes unveiling a new darkness that once imprisoned the truth.

The Sisters in the Deep Dark were bald. Not a follicle of hair sprouted from their clean-shaven scalps. They were kept bald, just as they were kept imprisoned. It had always been this way. No one could make sense of what they revealed, which was in fragments, slivers of information that were more often vital than useless. They had their collective finger on the figurative pulse of the stock market trends. They knew which politicians would become world leaders. This worked out greatly in the favor of their highly-connected captor. Pure and virginal. It was a travesty to take something so innocent and manipulate it for corrupt, amoral purposes.

An angelic choir stealing truth and spreading lies for the devil, resigned to a lifetime of captivity and subjugation. Strangely enough, the Sisters in the Deep Dark did not realize their situation. They were unsuspecting robots wearing flesh. Blood instead of coolant. Cold, methodical logic instead of expected human error. This was the way it was, the way it would always be. This was the norm.

Until *she* came.

The whisperings increased, a slow build-up, a mounting crescendo of the promise of something about to happen. The calm before the storm, before all hell broke loose. Then they all screamed once in perfect, blood-curdling unison. Some smacked or clutched their sweaty, alabaster domes. Others sobbed and spewed blood from biting their tongues. The metal chains connecting them shook and rattled as the sisters, for the first time, tried to stand up and flee.

The guard on monitor duty instantly notified the high-ranking official, the man in the dark-rimmed glasses, Emmanuel Snow.

It was Emmanuel's second or third time on that level. His duties primarily included assisting his boss, Amir Moradi, head of MalGenPro Labs. If his boss was a mover and shaker, then Emmanuel was the one who set things into motion. If his boss was considered an unstoppable machine, Emmanuel was the one who kept the cogs greased and oiled. He wore many hats, which made him the go-to contact when things needed to be done. A simple phone call prompted the quick withdrawal of his iPhone. And for this occasion, they needed him personally.

"Sir, you've gotta see this," the guard had said after Emmanuel swiped his ID badge, granting him admittance into the wing.

Emmanuel suppressed a slight smirk at being called "sir." That title was always used for his revered alpha, the emissary. He wore a pristine navy-blue suit made more vibrant by his blood-red tie, fastened in a timeless Windsor knot. He still looked all of eighteen years old, despite being twenty-seven. However, his appearance worked to his advantage whenever his peers and foes (which, more often than not, were one and the same) underestimated him.

"Lead the way, Jamison," Emmanuel said, unfazed by the long winding hallway and its sterile steel and white accents. No art adorned the walls. The hallway served a purpose. Lights set up at intervals illuminated their path until they reached an elevator. Emmanuel nodded his thanks when Jamison gestured for him to go first into the elevator.

"How is your day going, sir?" Jamison asked as they made their descent into the bowels of the MalGenPro Labs facility.

Emmanuel offered a side glance and brief smile. "As to be expected. Preparations for the new product, ReJuvenate, are well underway. The test subjects are responding well to their treatments. And let's see . . . I will be accompanying Mr. Moradi on his business trip to New Delhi for possible business ventures. But that is not what intrigues me right now. Tell me more about the psychics."

Jamison shook his head slowly, baffled. "It's like nothing I've ever seen. Normally, we see them chanting and muttering from our monitors. But then, five minutes ago, there was a spike in the readings, and our live stream showed them going crazy." He shuddered in his heavy-duty impact vest and fatigues. "It was disturbing, sir."

Emmanuel bit his lip, a trait he had developed during childhood whenever something piqued his interest, and this interested him greatly. "Fascinating. The sisters have been in captivity for several years now, and this has never happened before. Well, let's see what they have to say."

They stopped before a stainless-steel door. Beside it was a crimson light from a retina scanner. It chirped as it read Emmanuel's eyes. The door slid open with a hydraulic hiss. A sliver of cold light parted the darkness before them. Moans of agony and torment wafted out like a diseased aroma. Jamison hung back. The Sisters in the Deep Dark unnerved him, as they did most people. Unfazed, Emmanuel stepped inside.

A heaviness descended on him like a blanket covered in crawling ants. It pricked and stung him, suffocated him. Emmanuel found himself absently scratching the back of his hand and behind his ear before he realized it was the sisters' agitation in semi-tangible form. Their fear and confusion was palpable. Emmanuel closed his eyes to for a moment, centering himself, before he braced for the mental anguish that the shackled sisters were broadcasting.

"She is coming, she is here. She is coming, she is here . . ."

They repeated the words on a loop.

He stepped in deeper. For a moment, they did not notice him, whispering their unending lament through raw, liquid voice boxes. Even in the dark, he could make out the glistening blood on their chins.

Emmanuel knelt beside the cushion upon which the youngest sister sat. Her head was bowed, and she swayed from side to side. Hot tears trickled down her puffy cheeks. Her little shoulders heaved up and down. Slowly, she raised her head to stare unflinchingly into his eyes. "She has returned," she croaked in a voice that should never have sounded from the lips of one so young. Her pupils matched the red, broken veins in the whites of her eyes.

Emmanuel pursed his lips, withdrew a handkerchief from his breast pocket, and dabbed at her swollen cheeks. She barely registered the act of kindness. Instead, she rattled on, her sisters' sobbing and moaning serving as a backdrop.

"The childless mother. The nameless one. The woman of many faces. The vessel is back for the first time."

Emmanuel stared intently at the bald child, his heartbeat picking up. He had a strong suspicion of whom she spoke. Could it be . . .?

"Her," the young girl said, plucking the question from this mind as if it were cotton candy. "Yes. The vessel is back. She will change everything."

"Where is she now?" Emmanuel asked, his heart racing.

The little girl reached for his hand, her lip trembling. He acquiesced. The child's fingertips barely brushed his hand before a wave of sensory information flooded his mind. He grunted and forced back a flash of nausea as he saw an image of a woman in churning waters rescued by a man. Emmanuel was able to make out the name on the shrimp trawler: *Peaches*. Then the scene cut to a small bar, where the two people sat. Was it Cyrus? Cyrus Dhandi. Indeed, it was. And then the final scene—a hospital room, where she slept restlessly. Then the image burst like a soap bubble.

The albino child continued to sob.

Emmanuel ignored her as he stood up, dusting off his knees. A thin layer of sweat beaded his upper lip. It was finally happening. It was unfolding like the emissary had foreseen. They would have to be ready. Her death was of utmost concern. She would need to be eliminated before she remembered. He would have to inform the emissary at once. And yet...

Absently, he adjusted his tie before withdrawing his phone. He blinked as he dialed the number. "Ariadne? It's me, Emmanuel Snow. I have a task. It needs to be quick...and clean."

8

"So, when's the part where I get a lawyer?" Cyrus asked in a deadpan tone.

"I dunno," Sergeant Avis replied, a malicious gleam adding to his flabby scowl. "Do you think you need one?"

Cyrus did not bother to reply. He went to cross his arms but then realized his left arm was bandaged.

Sergeant Avis took the opportunity to dump a stack of documents on the small table. He'd left Detective Regan with the mysterious black woman with the weird blue eyes. He thought there was something creepy about her. He did not like looking in her eyes. Voodoo queen or some crap. He was all too happy when Regan suggested they have some "girl time." Sergeant Avis knew better. It would fall disappointingly short of his wicked and vivid imagination. Damn broads.

"That accent of yours is not from around these parts," he continued, hands flat on the table. He leaned forward, maintaining eye contact, his scowl deepening the crags and lines in his weathered face. His belly jiggled a little.

That last minor detail did not escape his prisoner. Cyrus had to bite the inside of his cheek to keep from bursting into laughter. Instead, he affected a nonchalant shrug. "No one is ever from around these parts. We come from all over."

Sergeant Avis smirked. Lifting his eyebrow, he pushed off the table and grabbed his paperwork. "Ain't that the truth! Mister

New Yorker with a rap sheet as long as my—"

"I wouldn't finish that sentence, if I were you. Let's not compare each other," Cyrus interjected, hand raised, eyes closed. "Irish curse and all."

The heavyset cop roared and took a swing at him. Cyrus reacted quickly, but just barely, causing Avis to miss. A slow, easy grin found its way back to Cyrus's face. He did not feel like having his past recited to him. Not now. Not ever. There was a reason why the past was called the past. And yet, Avis continued.

"You won't get off that easy, you little turd," the cop said, squinting as he held Cyrus's rap sheet. "Your life of petty crime started in the USA. Mostly New York. Burglary, robbery, petty larceny. Oh! Looks like you did most of this before you turned twenty-one." Avis laughed as he shook his head, eyes still narrowed. "Worthless, really. But your last name . . ." His voice trailed off as he realized something.

Cyrus's heart began to hammer in his chest. He knew this day would come. It was only a matter of time before everything he had striven to put behind him reared its head once again.

Then the hairs on the back of his neck stood up. The energy in the room shifted, yet, the temperature remained the same. Cyrus looked at Avis and was relieved to see that the poor excuse of a cop felt it too. It was the pressure of a storm building, unseen but felt. With growing horror, he watched Avis's pupils dilate then change color entirely.

Avis shuddered several times then rolled his neck. Bones popped loudly. He blinked and looked around the room in wonderment. His movement was deliberate and achingly slow. Cyrus stifled a chill. The rotund officer's red eyes pulsed with unnerving intensity. They zeroed in on Cyrus. "The fisherman," he uttered in a voice that seemed to echo and be layered all at once. The voice did not belong to his body.

Panic and puzzlement registered on Cyrus's face. Fisherman? What was with his voice? He glanced at the door. Could he make it out in time? Was it locked? He turned back to the cop. "Avis?"

Avis responded by cracking his knuckles and staring at the back of his hand. His eyes rolled back to Cyrus, and a broad smile broke out across his face. It was like a disease, sick and all encompassing. "No, fisherman, this officer with the bad breath and even worse thoughts is momentarily screaming in the dark pits of his mind. We have taken over."

"We?" Cyrus asked, drawn in despite himself. "We who?"

"We Sisters of the Deep Dark," the voice replied, sounding like a dry wind rustling through leaves. "Oracles of divine truth and purpose. We see it all happen before it happens. We know the secrets of your heart. We give voice to your sins, the sins acted out and the ones thought of in wicked silence. We—"

"I get it," Cyrus said. The longer he was involved with the mysterious woman, the stranger his life was becoming. He was surrendering to it. In just one day, he had gone toe to toe with a monster, and now he was talking to a possessed police officer. What next? He had a sinking suspicion as to where this was going, but he was helpless to stop it. Still, they needed to know this. He puffed out his chest and willed himself forward. "So, what now, my possessed jailer?"

"Now we make sure you are fit for transport," they whispered in a voice that sounded like many. "Our benefactor was delighted to discover you were involved in her arrival. He truly was. And after the failed banshee sanction, the emissary wants to take matters into his own hands."

Cyrus stared at the table. It was too much to process. Too much hopelessness, bewilderment, and a new dose of fear. Sisters in the Deep Dark? Transport? And who in the hell was this emissary person? He looked up at Avis. "Is this the part where you say, 'resistance is futile'?"

The possessed police officer twisted the corner of his mouth upward in a mockery of a grin. "No, Cyrus Dhandi. The gift of divination is not yours to wield. You do not see events tomorrow like we do. But she has disrupted the flow and must be dealt with accordingly. You both will. But first we need to make you a little more agreeable."

Avis's eyes flared as he hissed. Then black tendrils of psionic power reached across the table for Cyrus.

****

"I don't think you're listening."

The woman with no name looked up, guilty as charged. Her mind raced with exit possibilities. Staying there was not an option. She had to find the scribe. Could he help her? If so, where to start?

She squinted as a wave of apprehension settled over her. Something was amiss. A change had just occurred, like a drop in air pressure. The prickling of goosebumps on her flesh. Malevolent tidings trickled into the interrogation room like an odorous pall, filmy and cloying. The smell of decaying flowers, pungent and too sweet; the fall of black snow, silent but no less abnormal. The flavor of a sick hive mind.

Different eyes blinked at her. Detective Regan was no longer in control of her body. The nameless woman straightened up in her seat, eyes alert and wary as Regan grinned in a way that did not look right on a human face. She winked.

The nameless woman bristled. She got the distinct impression the officer knew what she was just thinking. The energy the officer emanated felt wrong—diseased and depraved, full of malice and melancholy blowing on a putrid wind. A wind with greedy fingers reaching out to her, wishing to grab and molest and rend. Chittering and whispering on the edge of sanity, blinking eyes in the shadows. Sixteen pairs of eyes watching from the darkness. But first it had to breach her defenses. Somehow, she could see this beneath the mask of Regan's face, the invisible visitors using the detective as a puppet. With a set jaw, she watched Regan take profound delight in the hem of her blazer.

"What do you want?" she finally hissed through gritted teeth.

Detective Regan looked up and gave a creepy smile that would have made the Cheshire Cat disappear. "We had to see for ourselves. We needed to see Eternity's Daughter with our own eyes. You have no idea how dead others wish you to be." The smile grew wider still.

"Eternity's Daughter?" she echoed, her curiosity piqued despite everything. "Why do you want me dead? Why do others want me dead?"

The smile on Regan's face flashed with anger. "Yes, woman of many faces. You manifested and nearly short-circuited the sacred bond between my sisters and me."

"Clearly I didn't do a very good job," she countered, sarcasm thick and heavy. Questions abounded in her mind, but for every question she asked, more questions popped up, followed by few answers. And yet her arrival must have done some good, considering the pure malice the possessed entity emitted. Maybe, just maybe, they needed to be stopped. The old man had said a great darkness was coming. And it didn't get much darker than possession and the unique, indescribable aura of a diseased mind. Somehow, she knew a hive mind was controlling Regan but—

She froze.

A hive mind was more than just one controller. And if they easily took over Regan . . .

"Sergeant Avis," she whispered, her voice full of dread. Cyrus was in danger. The realization made her stomach churn. This was the preamble to an attack. "He's not in control. Just like Detective Regan."

Detective Regan shrugged nonchalantly, checking her nails. "They are no longer the people you were once acquainted with. Their minds are being hollowed out, even as we speak, consumed by my sisters and me. Broken vessels who were not meant to hold our psychic power. But you, the fabled vessel, on the other hand . . ."

A feral look flashed in the nameless woman's eyes, challenging and threatening. "You're welcome to try."

The bewitched officer with dead eyes let out a sorrowful sigh. "You would be delicious to sup on. But we have our orders. You and the fisherman are to return with us. And our lord, the emissary, will not wait long."

The nameless woman rose from her seat, fists clenched at her side. "I'm not going anywhere with you."

Detective Regan smiled. "Silly broken vessel, it has already begun!"

Vertigo.

Nausea.

She lost control of her bearings and did not know whether she was falling or still seated in the uncomfortable chair. Laughter from the murky depths, all-encompassing as she was thrust backward. Again, she was unsure if the sensation was real or not. A tiny part of her remembered that multiple psychics crowded the mind of not just Regan but most likely the one interrogating Cyrus in the other room.

Shards of images splintered her vision, encircled her, crashed against her as she continued to fall backward, legs kicking, hands clawing at nothing. It did not take her long to realize she was screaming during the plunge, which reminded her of hitting the cold, chilling water that had stolen her life. The memory whispered to her from the cracks of reality, begging her to remember, entreating her to know who she was. Whoever wanted her dead gained from her confusion, her broken sense of self. It was his power; he had leverage. And that knowledge, that sickening, stomach-churning knowledge burrowed into her heart, her soul, like a worm inside an apple.

Silly, broken vessel.

Eternity's Daughter.

And out there was the scribe, the one person who could help her.

Must gain control, she thought, forcing herself to get her bearings. She had not realized her eyes were closed until she opened them. A barren, lifeless landscape devoid of life. Of hope. Sand blew hot and scorching across her bare feet. And across from her was Detective Regan—or what was left of her.

The body was recognizable. The hollowed cheeks. Ash-blond hair pulled into a no-nonsense ponytail. But those eyes . . . as black as sin and sometimes red with rage. Flickering, chameleon-like, promising untold pain and destruction. But if she looked closer, she saw a well of suffering that went so deep attempting to alleviate it would draw her into it and steal her life with icy fingers dipped in death.

Seven images of bald women hovered around her form, wavering and indistinct, much like the heat wavering from the hard-packed earth.

"Where are we?" she asked, her hands balled into fists at her sides. A wind blew tufts of her shoulder-length natural hair.

What was left of Detective Regan gestured theatrically. "We are no longer on the physical plane. We are in your mind, and this is how you envision it." Her lip curled into a mocking sneer. "Not a whole lot to work with. But then, that's no surprise."

"Funny, considering you want to take over my body."

"Blank canvas and all."

"Are we going to continue shooting the breeze or get down to it? You have no idea how unhealthy and sick your aura is."

The sisters hissed angrily and charged at an impossible speed. She barely had time to block the first of several attacks. They were surprisingly strong. But she was stronger. Anger strengthened the uppercut she delivered, followed by a swift knee to the groin. She moved without thinking. Thought and motion were one, made fluid in her mind's eye. Regan growled and caught the next blow before head-butting the nameless woman.

She staggered back, stars bursting in her eyes and melting in her vision. That was all the sisters needed. They pressed their attack, cursing, laughing, sobbing, howling like unnatural creatures as they hungered to dominate her body and drag it back, screaming and kicking, to their master. One moment, they sounded like a little schoolgirl playing in a pool of blood. The next moment, like a throaty, enticing seductress laughing over the remains of her lover, whom she had shot to death. And then the high-pitched cackle of hyenas circling a wounded gazelle dripping its life away into the red dirt. She would not be that gazelle.

She swung—and missed. Then she took a fist to her face. The blow sent tremors of pain rippling across her body. She tried to stand, but a side kick sent her spinning into the dirt. Blood ran hot and fast down her forehead, blinding her. Her lips were bruised and bloody, like overripe fruit. At least her blood would quench her thirst in that dry, dead world.

"Do you understand how small you are?" The sisters asked before licking a bloody knuckle. "The banshee was ill-equipped to deal with you, but here in the ruin of your mind, we reign supreme. Your mind and your thoughts are ours to twist, rip, and devour. We hold the power, the true power. Now kneel!"

Power.

On all fours, she remembered the old man, his cryptic advice, and his dark portents of the future. But he had also imparted something else.

"I just needed you to know that you have great power, and to discover who you are and to stop the tidal wave of darkness that is about to wash over you."

She grabbed a fistful of dirt.

"Reconcile who you were with who you will be. Therein lies your gift."

She rose shakily to her feet.

Eyes aglow, like a star burning in intensity, she recalled the cool, dank cave. The drip of water from the stalagmites. It centered her, empowered her. In that moment, she drew the connection to what the shaman had hinted at. She knew what fit. Better yet, it was getting easier to access it. Finally, a connective ribbon. It was time to reconcile the past with the present to save the future.

"You messed with the wrong one."

The arid, lifeless landscape shifted to a vast ocean. The waves were black and impenetrable. Chunks of rock broke the choppy surface. Her bare feet hovered over one rock. Her eyes were shut tight and her hands outstretched. The familiar sensation returned, icy energy that brought a tingly feeling, like blood circulating through a limb that had fallen asleep. And, in truth, her limbs, her body, her soul had been asleep for too long. Answers were a long way off. Her memory was still a jumbled mess. But this strange, wondrous power? It was hers. And she would use it once again (always at the height of great stress) to fight back the tidal wave of darkness. A knowing grin spread across her face. That shaman and his riddles.

Then, without warning, she raised both hands as if conducting an orchestra. In response, obelisks of water punched from the ocean's depths and reached for the sky. Her eyes snapped open, pulsing brightly, pupil-less, lost in the flow of untapped power, her birthright and her special gift. Adrenaline felt like a drug as the power surged in her mind. The Sisters in the Deep Dark were wrong. How could they hold power in the mind of one such as her? She reigned supreme over her shattered kingdom. Broken as it was, it still belonged to her and no one else!

Hydrokinesis.

Somewhere, somehow, across the annals of space and time, so many eons removed, she felt rather than saw the wizened old man part his cracked lips into a smile.

"*Little sparrow.*"

She matched his smile with her own.

She directed a swirling obelisk of water into the . . . "soul-eater." Yes, an appropriate name for the enemy who had invaded her mind. They preyed on weak wills, on unprotected minds. Luckily for her, she was strengthening simply because it was necessary. As much as Cyrus thought he was protecting her, she was protecting him. That thought alone increased the fervor of her attack.

She defied gravity, flying toward the drowning figure. They could not scream audibly, but in that realm, she heard it just the same. Their eyes locked. Regan slammed on the cage made of water rising from the sea. The nameless one waved her hand, and a window opened so her prisoner could breathe. Regan took a shuddering gasp and inhaled the oxygen greedily.

"Ready to behave?"

Regan replied with a series of rapid nods.

"I don't know why I'm being targeted, and at this moment, I don't care. Tell the emissary, or whatever his name is, to leave me alone. Stop coming after me and my friend!"

Still hovering mid-air, pillars of water bracketing them both in that world of sea and shadow, she pictured the interrogation room in detail. She gasped as she snapped her eyes open. She was back, but swirling bands of water snaked around her. Regan was coughing up water on the floor, soaked to the bone.

As if in a trance, the nameless woman walked past her. The flick of her wrist sent an animated water coil into the door, blasting it off its hinges. She walked slowly, ignoring the shouts of the officers converging on her. A wall of water rose just in time to absorb their bullets.

The door leading to Cyrus's interrogation room met a fate similar to her own. Cyrus stood there in confusion. Avis was on his knees, coughing up water. She smiled faintly and then locked eyes with Cyrus. The color drained from his cheeks, and his eyes widened.

"Y-you're doing it again," he stammered.

She could not relinquish her hold on her gift. She still had to do one more thing. "Take my hand," she beseeched, reaching out with her luminous hand. Neon veins pulsed in her arm and throughout her body. She stepped closer. He stepped back. The officers' angry cries drew closer.

"B-but what's going on? What *are* you?" Cyrus was having a mini breakdown. He was only human. And she was something else.

"I am something . . . more," she whispered in a voice of ice and flame, far older than the face she wore. An unnatural wind kept her long locks afloat. "Trust me, as I have trusted you."

"Oh, man," Cyrus said, overwhelmed. Indecision and cold feet kept him rooted in place. His mouth parted into an "O" of surprise when the cops clustered around the door, guns aimed. "Is it too late to go back to *Peaches?*"

She smiled as they clasped hands. "I'm afraid so, Cyrus. Hold on!"

As the policemen opened fire, a pulsating, aquatic portal ripped into existence. Crisp, cool, churning waves of energy formed a tunnel to a destination far from there. One word was burned into her mind as she prayed to whatever god was listening that they would make it. They took one last look at each another before jumping through. The first bullet bit into the wall as the portal closed, taking its two inhabitants to parts unknown.

9

"So, uh, how are you feeling?"

"Well, you know, I was just thrashed around by a banshee, then I had my brain attacked by some albino hive mind. Oh, and then I hopped in a water portal."

"You didn't answer the question."

"You're right; I didn't. Sorry. I'm cool."

She turned to him, one eyebrow raised, before turning away, shaking her head. The addictive power that kept her floating and telekinetically controlling water had left her shaky and exhausted. Her last feat—the water portal—had left her utterly drained. She felt a faint echo in her soul, a lingering ache. She missed it, along with the boost of confidence it instilled in her whenever she tapped into that source. She looked out across San Francisco Bay at the Golden Gate Bridge. She remembered the portal ripping through reality not far from the shoreline before unceremoniously dumping them in the waist-deep water. Despite her injuries, she helped Cyrus to shore. He was in worse shape than her and was still affected by the psychic attack of the Sisters of the Deep Dark. He had complained about a migraine. That was approximately ten minutes earlier.

They rested and caught their breath, still attired in Salvation Army hand-me-downs. Not that they cared. They just needed a few minutes to collect themselves before taking their next step—whatever that might be.

"I see..." She raked a hand through her massive mane of curls. She felt she could fall asleep right there, but a nervous energy kept her from lying on her back and closing her eyes. Instead, she turned back to Cyrus. He, too, appeared tired but restless. Dark rings encircled his chartreuse eyes. His gangly profile showed off his narrow nose with the slight hook at the end. The pink tip of his tongue darted out to moisten his lips. He must have felt her looking at him because he turned, flushing slightly.

"What?"

She shook her head, smiling softly. "Nothing, it's just that . . . so much has happened. I feel like we're war-hardened soldiers, yet the simple luxury of me knowing my name seems like an impossibility." The thread of aggravation was hard to mask.

"Hey, go easy on yourself," he said, his voice deep and raspy. It pulled at a tiny invisible thread in her stomach. She squirmed uncomfortably. He was oblivious. "I won't pretend I know what's going on," he continued, "I won't even say this doesn't scare me on some level. You scare me."

She jerked. "What? I didn't mean to scare you."

Cyrus threw up his hands. "No! Wait. I suck at this. It's just that you seem normal now, but you were floating on hospital beds and controlling water. That is the utter opposite of normal!"

She could not disagree. "Yes, I suppose it is."

For the first time in what seemed like ages, she felt shame. Shame at her shortcomings and stunted progress in her journey despite the physical distance they had covered. What had she truly accomplished? Were the Sisters in the Deep Dark right? A blank canvas of . . . what? Thoughtfully, she massaged a spot on her chest.

"So, it is real," she heard Cyrus say in a far-off voice.

She looked down and saw she was rubbing a tattoo. It was unique, a phoenix interlocked with an ankh. Traced in smoldering oranges and blue. It felt tingly on her fingertips. "Yes, and it seems to flare up when I use my powers."

Cyrus turned to her. "About that. Like I said, scary, but so freakin' awesome!" His face lit up like a kid in a candy store, and the corners of his eyes crinkled merrily. "I must confess, I'm a little jealous."

She scoffed. "Trust me. You don't want this. You don't want to be . . . different. Not like this."

His smile wilted slightly. "I guess. But I'm no stranger to feeling like that."

Curiosity caused her eyebrows to rise. "Really?" A thought nagged at her, one that had been lurking in the back of her head for hours. She let it float to the forefront of her mind. "It appears I'm not the only mystery present. I have a valid reason for not knowing what's going on. I have no secrets to divulge. Can you say the same?"

Cyrus's nostrils flared, and he clenched his teeth. Then, just like that, the flash of indignation was gone. If anything, he seemed resigned as the tension left his shoulders. "Honestly, no, I can't."

He let his words linger for a moment. She waited patiently. It was the least she could do considering how patient he had been.

Cyrus sighed. "I never fit in with my family. The 'black sheep' in the family portraits, ya know? I was supposed to run the family business, but there was no way I could do it. I felt like I was drowning, so I did some things, some bad things, to try to escape in any way I could."

Silence, heavy and pregnant, loomed between them.

"I haven't told you yet," she said, "but I've seen this old man twice now."

Cyrus bit his bottom lip, curious. "What do you mean?"

She brought her knees to her chest and held her legs tight. "I first saw him when I was sleeping, right before we docked. Then when I was sleeping during the banshee attack, somehow, I made contact with him. He said I 'time-slipped' by dreaming. Said I had to save you and find the scribe."

Cyrus opened his mouth to say something and then closed it. "So, this old dude knew you?"

"Seems like it."

"So, that's good news, right?"

She shrugged. "It's a start."

"You don't seem too enthused about it."

She could tell he knew she had held something back. She sighed and straightened her left leg, staring straight ahead. "It's something. But I need more. Like, where do we start?"

Cyrus chuckled. "We?"

She whipped her head toward him, a smile teasing her lips. "Yes, 'we.' Unless you don't want to go."

Shaking his head, Cyrus reached for her hand. She withdrew it impulsively. He flushed slightly, dusted off his legs, and stood up. "We've already spilled blood, and I'm determined to see this to the end." He looked down at her. "Aren't you?"

She gazed up at him as she rubbed the hand he had touched. She had so much to say, and yet the words remained lodged in her throat—the ones that mattered anyway. "Yes. And thank you."

He reached for her hand again. "Need help getting up?"

She nodded and allowed him to pull her to her feet. For the first time, she looked in his eyes, truly looked. Pools of chartreuse light, mischievous and welcoming. The adventure, the risk, and the danger spoke to him, distracted him. She could see that now. In truth, she could not push him away even if she tried. She did not want him to push though. The longer they stayed together, the more at ease she felt. That scared her. Despite everything, all she wanted to do was lay her head against his chest.

"You can if you want to," she heard him murmur into her unruly hair.

Sighing, she closed her eyes and leaned against him, inhaling his rich masculine scent, the only thing that seemed real in her life of constant flux. Tension evaporated from her. She welcomed the arm he wrapped around her, drawing her closer. She could tell he was nervous too. Was this what a new friendship was about? Hugs after life-and-death experiences?

"Hey . . ."

Eyes closed, she whispered a reply, lower and huskier than intended. "Yeah?"

"We really need a name for you."

She pulled back and looked up at him, a smile painted on her face. "I agree. You choose."

Cyrus lifted an eyebrow. "Seriously?"

"Seriously."

"Okay then." Cyrus looked up, then moved his lips to the

side. "How about . . ."

"Finally!"

They both turned toward the voice.

A petite woman of Asian descent waved excitedly at them. She was a lot to take in—a pink-frosted fauxhawk complimented dark eyeshadow. An old, bulky leather jacket hugged her small shoulders. Colorful buttons and pins decorated the lapel. Plaid mini-skirt over ripped stockings and combat boots. Car keys jangled in her grip as she made her way toward them, a unicorn keychain dangling to and fro. Lipstick, hot and pink like cake icing, painted her lips as they pulled back into a wide grin. Huge black-framed glasses completed the look.

They stared numbly as she closed the small distance between them with a massive bear hug. "So glad you guys made it out alive!"

They winced from their respective injuries as the stranger gave them a squeeze. "Do you know us?" the woman inquired. Cyrus was bewildered into silence.

"Oh no! Not yet!" The newcomer laughed and released them, both still out of breath. "There's a lot of ground to cover. And we will! Let's get you guys back to my place first. You guys want bubble tea on the way?"

Cyrus snapped to life and held up his hands. "Wait, wait, wait! Who are you? And why should we trust you?"

For the first time since happening on the scene, the woman took a breath and seemed to slow down. "Oh my God; I totally suck. My name is Ramona Li. A pleasure. I'm the scribe."

****

Fighting for one's life was hungry work. This fact was becoming clear to the mysterious duo. They said little as Ramona prattled on about miscellaneous things as she drove her beat-up, old-fashioned hearse, a 1970 Cadillac. At a speed that would leave even a bumblebee dazed and confused, Ramona jumped from the latest novels to the latest movies to the best pizza in San Francisco.

". . . but it doesn't top New York pizza. I mean, oh my gawd."

She tittered as she turned to face the speechless duo, then paused to take a breath. "But I'm not hungry for that. I could go for a greasy burger and a milkshake, ya dig? You guys like meat and dairy, right? I mean, you aren't vegan police because if you want to go the Tropical Smoothie or somewhere else . . ."

"No, it's cool," Cyrus replied, flashing a quick glance in the elemental's direction. "Hamburgers would be great right now. Do you have a place in mind?"

Ramona grinned broadly. "Hell freckin' yeah!"

The Goodie Box had seen better days. Just off the corner of Clement Street, it was a small relic of times gone by. Faded awning. Paint bleached and peeling from the door. It was a small "greasy spoon" that kicked awake the hunger lying dormant in their empty bellies. Fried foods and sugary drinks to clog the arteries and bring back gout with a vengeance. No wonder it was packed!

They had parked in the back. Ramona was lucky enough to get a spot when a couple reversed their Honda Accord and inched out onto the road. She led the way much like a tour guide going for a punk vibe. She pushed open the door and ushered them inside. She waved to a few patrons and then shuffled toward the back of the diner, where a booth was unoccupied.

"They have the best chili fries here," she gushed, eyes twinkling.

The nameless woman slid into the booth facing Ramona, Cyrus at her side. "I don't think I've ever had them."

"You can totally have some of mine," Ramona offered. She waved, and a waitress bustled over to them. "Hey, Stella!"

Stella was a middle-aged woman of African American descent. She was bow-legged, and when she walked, she favored her left leg. Her skin was a dusky brown, and she had slight crows' feet but no other visible signs of aging. She was stout and full-bodied, bordering on chubby but not overweight. Her uniform's white collar was stained with grease. A smile that rivaled Ramona's spread across her face. "How y'all doin'? Welcome to the Goodie Box!"

The nameless woman felt the beginnings of a smile. The accent was definitely southern. Wrong for that region, and yet it seemed right at home amidst the endearing, mouth-watering aroma of deep-fried meats, crackling grease (no doubt popping the cook slaving in the back with sweat stains under his armpits and neckline), and the strong, commanding scent of brewing coffee. Perhaps she had come with the place, a timeless staple of its wares and services, a throwback to the way things were.

They greeted her in unison. Cyrus stared at her in silent awe.

Stella smacked her gum and withdrew a pen from behind her ear. "Now y'all know we're the best diner in all of San Fran, right? No? Well, you do now! We have a blue-plate special, a really good deal for y'all who want a quality meal but don't want to spend an arm and a leg—or some feet!" She laughed at her own joke, loud and braying. "We're offering French onion soup, some beef brisket, mashed potatoes, and macaroni and cheese so good you'll stomp your foot and slap your mama!"

Cyrus burst out laughing. The nameless woman shook her head, more amused than she should have been.

"Y'all need some more time? If so, then that's wonderful!"

The woman who had just been reborn mere hours ago nodded. "More time would be wonderful. In fact, can you provide us with menus?"

Stella chuckled as if her patron with the Diana Ross hair had just said the funniest thing ever. "Girl, you a mess. I'll be back in two shakes with them menus."

"Water, too, please."

Stella sauntered away before stopping at another patron's table to see if they wanted anything else.

Cyrus and the woman looked at Ramona expectantly. She seemed to have all the answers, and there was no time like the present. "So, how did you know we were looking for the scribe?" the nameless woman asked. Every word was laden with suspicion. It did not pay to be naïve, especially when lives depended on it.

For the first time since she had scooped them up from San Francisco Bay, Ramona's expression turned serious. And for a moment, the nameless woman regretted her words. Ramona had seemed so lively and brought such an infectious energy. She could see it as if it were an aura. Perhaps it was. Now that her bright, contagious energy had dampened, the room seemed bigger, less welcoming. How odd that the girl with the crazy colored hair and nonstop chatter would affect her so. She seemed like a unique if not a kindred spirit. Just the same, answers would be nice.

"Well, since you asked so nicely," Ramona replied, hands clasped in front of her, "I knew simply because I've dreamed it for the last few nights now. I kept seeing a woman in water, dying, all CGI special effects-ish. She was glowing and was in so much pain..."

Cyrus looked at the nameless woman. She let out a soft sound somewhere between a sigh and a gasp. A tingly sensation prickled the hairs on her neck. She recalled her meeting the old man in the cave. He was the one who had told her to seek out the scribe.

"That woman was me—is me. Cyrus saved me in Australia. You dreamed of me."

Ramona bunched her eyebrows. "Australia? Then how did you get here?"

The nameless woman and Cyrus exchanged a look. Cyrus coughed. "You want the crazy truth or a lie?"

"Fact is stranger than fiction," Ramona replied. "Try me."

"By portal. A portal made of water. A water portal."

Ramona nodded slowly, impressed. "That's pretty rad. I always knew there were such people out there in the world. Special people with special abilities."

Before the others could reply, Stella sauntered over with three battered menus. She smiled as she set them before each member of the party. "I'll give y'all some more time, okay? Look over our awesome selection." She glided away to refill coffee mugs and take new orders as the chatter around them swelled in volume. They were happy for the privacy.

Ramona looked around conspiratorially and then leaned closer. Cyrus and the nameless woman did so as well. "I'm a bit of a nerd. I do tons of reading. Like towers and towers of books for leisure and research. I own a small book café. It's my haven, my watchtower. We can talk about everything there. Plus, it's safer." She looked around. They did too. The other patrons continued to talk, but suddenly, the three of them felt out of place. Vulnerable. Targeted.

Stella finally returned, all apologies, but then stopped mid-sentence when she saw the looks on their faces. "Whatsamatta?"

Ramona forced a smile, but it did not quite reach her eyes. "Stella, we're about to order, but can we have it to go?"

Stella laughed. "To go in one our famous Goodie Boxes? Sure thing! But remember it's really, really important to feel good, good, goodie at the Goodie Box!" She laughed at herself once again, and the others were polite enough to join in.

****

They were learning that with Ramona, there was never a direct route to their destination. There were always detours—brief pit stops filled with lively conversation that bordered on adolescent interests. When they agreed to swing by a thrift store to pick up clothing, they learned about the latest anime/manga conventions, the best cerebral shows to watch via online streaming, and her obsession with unicorns. She told them flat out that adulthood was boring, so she had to keep things lively. Her way of dressing and her obsession with books kept her aloof and different, icing on the cake.

The nameless woman idly trailed her fingers over the garments on the clothing racks. It had been a good idea to drop by, considering she and Cyrus were without clothing for the foreseeable future. Cyrus offered to pay, but Ramona insisted on paying for it. She said she could afford the merchandise on her budget.

Is it over? Can I take a breath? the mystery woman asked herself, fingering the beaded hemline of a peasant shirt. *It's been so crazy these past few hours. I just need to know, so I can stop looking over my shoulder.* She draped the top over her arm and eyed the other blouses and shirts. They had a vintage, earthy feel. *I sent the sisters back to tell him to leave us alone. Will it be enough? Can I just stay here until I figure out my next move? And if it's not over, am I strong enough to protect my new friends?*

She looked up and saw Ramona and Cyrus waist deep in a lively conversation about comic books.

"No way. X-Man was the most powerful mutant; his telepathy and his telekinesis could let him do almost anything!"

"Except see the future, like Sister Perpetua," Ramona said, stomping her booted foot in protest.

"Who in the world is Sister Perpetua?" he asked, laughing and gesturing dramatically.

The woman could not help but smile at the sight. Somehow, they had found a sliver of happiness, a moment of blissful forgetfulness amidst the drama that her life had dumped on them. The scribe and the fisherman, indeed. It seemed, at least according to the old man and recent events, that this was fated to be. Something bigger was happening. She played a big part in it and, to a certain extent, so did her allies. The puzzle was coming together, albeit agonizingly slow. Still, she watched them, arms crossed with the blouse tucked underneath, eyes glassy, some of the burden lifted off her shoulders. It was the pieces that unified the broken remnants of her soul, and unbeknownst to her until that moment, her heart. She belonged.

She held the garment closer and allowed herself a moment to sigh, eyes closed. Maybe it was over.

The bell above the door opened, and an elderly man ambled in. It was apparent immediately that he had been living on the streets for some time. His white beard, tightly-coiled and unclean, looked like dirty snow against a midnight sky. He wore a stained T-shirt and jeans that had more holes than cloth. Despite the heat, he also wore a patchwork blazer. One shaking hand clutched a tin that rattled with change.

Intrigued, she watched as he went from patron to patron, asking for money. The cashier, annoyed, swatted at him as if he were a fly. "Sir, you can't do that in here. Please, go." The cashier pursed her lips into a tight unforgiving line and crossed her arms. "I don't want to call the police."

They looked at each other, his hand still shaking. Then his gaze flitted from her to the nameless woman. A twinge moved a nerve above her eye. When he shuffled out of the store, surprisingly, at least to her, she followed. The bell chimed behind her as she caught up with him and touched his arm. "Sir?"

He turned slowly to face her. The move was familiar. Pinpricks of sensation washed over her. "Do . . . do I know you?"

He smiled. A faint scar across his face. "Little Sparrow. You are doing well, it seems."

Her heart pounded in her chest. "It's you!"

He chuckled. "Yes and no."

"But how?"

"Time is short," he said, avoiding her question. "You have them scared."

She smirked. "Well, that's good."

"No, that's very bad. Try to remember. Only then will you be truly prepared. And then when it all falls, you must choose."

"I don't understand. Can you give me more information?"

"You must choose," the old man repeated. "Nothing is as it seems."

"You okay?"

She turned around to find Cyrus and Ramona staring at her, puzzled. They were holding shopping bags.

"Who were you talking to?" Cyrus asked.

"The old man." She turned around and saw he was no longer there. "He was just here…"

They clustered around her. "C'mon," Cyrus said. "We gotta go, but first we gotta pay for that shirt."

She looked down and blushed. "Oh, right."

****

Ramona's book café, the aptly-named Writers' Block, proved to be a sanctuary not just for her but for all of them. It was small and unassuming. Easily forgettable for those driving past. But if on foot, one would be pulled into the quiet allure, the charm of the used-book store, which also provided affordable coffee.

"Come on in," Ramona said after unlocking the door, gesturing for the others to go in first. The smell of musty pages and hazelnut coffee greeted them. All senses were teased with the promise of something great, something old and venerable, knowledge and a cup of coffee hand in hand. A union most civil, the perfect marriage.

Cyrus stood to one side as the amnesiac elemental held her shopping bags. In the corner of her eye, she saw Ramona close the door. Writers' Block was overflowing with books—on shelves and stacked in waist-high towers. She was aware of the tight spaces, but claustrophobia did not come to mind.

"Nice place you got here," Cyrus said after a moment of silence. Looking around, he let his shopping bag slip to the floor beside a stack of encyclopedias that were probably older than him. "You aren't concerned about fire hazards?"

Ramona gasped and narrowed her eyes. She shouldered past him toward the counter. "Listen, Mr. Tall, Dark, and Uninformed, the place is not going to go up in flames!"

The nameless woman gave him a look before nudging him slightly, still aware of his injuries. "Really, Cyrus?"

He threw up his hands. "I'm sorry! I'm just saying!"

Ramona rolled her eyes. "Whatevs. Follow me. I have a small office, where I have my notes and stuff."

If the shop could be considered small, then her office was tiny. It was almost impossible how many books Ramona had crammed in there. Anime mixed in with classic movie posters covered all available wall space. Unicorn figurines and trinkets battled with open books and articles for space on her desk. The unicorns were losing. An old-fashioned PC took up most of the desk.

Cyrus looked around the room. "So, this is where old books come to die."

Both women stared him.

"Shutting up," he said, "starting now."

Rolling her eyes, their punk hostess indicated two chairs for them to sit. Once settled, she returned to the open book on her desk. She muttered to herself as she licked her index finger and thumb before turning through a few pages, occasionally looking over notes scrawled in a weathered spiral notebook. It was dog-eared and marked with color-coded tabs and a haphazard blend of marker and pen notations. "Do you have some sort of tattoo?" she asked randomly.

The mystery woman tore her gaze away from a book she had

spied in the corner. "Yes, I do. Why?"

"Like this?" Ramona pointed to a vintage sketch and spun the notebook toward them.

Cyrus allowed her to look first and then peered over her shoulder. He recognized the tattoo immediately. A phoenix and an ankh. Something about it seemed familiar. "I've seen something similar before," he said. "Like before I saw it on . . ." He paused and then nodded at his companion. "On our mystery girl here. It kinda looks like a phoenix."

Ramona looked up. "You're right. It's a very old symbol. Greek origins, but . . ." She picked up a pen from her desk and bit the end of it.

"I'm not Greek," the mystery woman replied. "Of that I'm pretty certain."

Ramona turned the page and then returned to the symbol. "Unless . . . no, wait. This makes sense."

The nameless woman peered over Ramona's shoulder. The longer she looked at the image, the more confused she became. They were so close. "What do you mean?"

"Okay, okay, you see this?" Ramona pointed to an illustration showing a bird rising from the flames. "That's a more common depiction of the phoenix. But look here." She turned the page to another image of a bird, a hieroglyphic rendition of a heron. It was stylized much like the bird on the woman's chest. "Bennu. Bennu was similar to the phoenix."

The nameless woman furrowed her brow. "Bennu isn't Greek though." Somehow, she knew that.

Ramona placed her pen on the table, a grin dancing across her face. "Ancient Egypt."

The nameless woman's knees wobbled a bit. She felt Cyrus's hand on her shoulder to steady her. She was grateful. She turned her head and nodded, as if to indicate she was okay. She felt him reluctantly withdraw his hand.

"Thank you, Cyrus."

"Don't mention it," he replied, moving in closer to get a better look. He narrowed his eyes. "It does look more like your tattoo. But so what?"

Ramona waved her hand at Cyrus to back up. "It means I have a sneaking suspicion." Ramona turned to the woman. "If it's okay, may I see your tattoo?"

"Of course." She lowered her shirt to reveal it. Ramona peered at it with the keen vision of a hawk. Cyrus did everything in his power not to stare. The image of him looking everywhere but her breast would have been comical if he had also begun to whistle. He backpedaled, bumping into a pile of books. It teetered. He tried to stop it from swaying. He was fortunate.

"That's it, alright." Ramona took a deep breath and crossed her arms, biting the corner of her mouth. She glanced at her books, her notes, and then at her guests.

The nameless woman's heart began to pound. She licked her lips. "What are you saying?"

Ramona flipped to a yellowed article in her notebook. Then another. She pointed out the hauntingly familiar image. "Like I said earlier, I dreamed about you in the water. I've had that dream for days now. Never had a face though. Just knew you were coming, so I had to be prepared, you know?"

The nameless woman swallowed hard. Sweat gathered on her upper lip. "But what about my tattoo? What does it mean?"

Ramona looked at her and then at Cyrus, who was positioned close to his companion. "It means that tattoo has been around a long time. My research says it goes back five hundred years!"

The nameless woman's heart pounded, heat rolling in waves across her flesh.

Reluctantly, Ramona pressed on. "It usually pops up on a woman whenever something is about to happen. Something bad. Eyewitnesses talk of seeing that tattoo first, but it usually fades when the woman dies."

What little protection she had been feeling was breaking up into tiny shards of glass, self-confidence splintering into the either. Her identity, a miasma of raw, unclenching pain that felt like liquid fire behind her eyes. In response, she felt the damned tattoo flare to life.

On the floor.

She was suddenly on the floor.

Voices in the distance. Muted and lost in the echoes of her pain. Tears finally came. Exhaustion caught up with her. Every harrowing second from her resurrection, from being pulled from the waves alongside dead fish to fighting a banshee to a mental battle with albino psychics. It all came crashing down upon her.

She wasn't meant to stop the tidal wave of darkness.

She was the darkness.

"My gift . . ." she said between body-shaking sobs. Too many hands on her in an attempt to comfort. "My gift . . . is death. I bring death with my powers. And no one is safe. Not even you two."

Then the darkness claimed her.

10

She stared, and a woman stared back. She was heavyset, and her eyes held equal amounts of a child's joy and the harsh realities of adulthood. Her hair was pulled back into a simple ponytail. She wore a tank top over loose-fitting pants. Her huge breasts were supported by a bra purchased from Lane Bryant. A cigarette dangled precariously between her pressed lips. Ashes drifted down like snow, flakes of cinder to coat the linoleum floor.

She was a woman.

A daughter.

A sister.

A mother.

And at that moment, she stared in the mirror, stared deep into her eyes.

The gorgon stared back.

She remained rooted in place, unflinching. An earthbound angel full of contradictions, tangled wings, and obligatory roles assigned to her. Children, lively and vocal, were the animated backdrop in the dead of summer. Heat, humid and bordering on oppressive, made her irritable, like the embrace of an overly affectionate lover. If she could have pushed it away or swatted at it, she would have.

She brought her fingertips to the bathroom mirror. A sigh caused the cigarette to tremble and let loose more ashes. The child's cry rang out, followed by more wailing. The woman shook her head and then withdrew from the mirror. A mother's work was never done. She left the room without looking back.

Heat. Hot and all consuming. It rose in lazy, invisible swirls from the hard-packed earth through the soles of her feet. It clogged her pores, adding a layer of misty dew upon her supple skin, the color of burnished mahogany. She smelled of sweat and sandalwood. There was no breeze. She was used to it.

The sun, an angry, flaming eye, kept her in its line of vision, never breaking its gaze. No clouds obscured the sun's unwavering glare. Perhaps they were scared. Who could say?

A basket was balanced perfectly atop her head, providing merciful shade from the unforgiving sun. She paid it no mind. The dirt road was before her. And she had a long way to go.

Bits of meaty flesh, putrid and decayed, slid down her face and off her tunic. She walked slowly, smelling of wet death, the blood streaking her body and clothing. Most of it was not hers. Her pupils were lost to a cyan blaze that was just losing its intensity. Bare feet crunched on the gravel. In her wake were the remains of those who wished to attack her. She kept walking.

The oversized hood did not offer much protection as the rain soaked it. Robust raindrops streamed down her face. One drop in particular hovered perilously on the tip of her nose before taking the fatal plunge. Her cloak trailed in the mud. Her bottom lip trembled, and her teeth chattered, not from the cold but from grief. No one knew the rain was washing away her tears. She was so sorry.

So very sorry, indeed.

Were these memories? Each one had such a different flavor, a different... life. Life? She continued to float through the ether of her confusion, given semi-tangible form, a steady stream of slivers of an identity that had remained out of reach for the better part of her life, her new life since Cyrus had saved her. But from what? Where had she been before? Why was she the woman with many faces? Why did she lack a name? Who was she? Something dark, something powerful. Something evil.

Had the banshee been right?

Then there was Ramona and her books and research that catalogued the nameless woman's exploits for the last five hundred years! But these women were so different, each one with a story uniquely her own. Ranging from idle observation of one's self to being covered in the blood of one's enemies. Slow death by seconds in sun-scorched suburbia to the high-pitched blood song of a blade and maddening rage. Single moms and single warriors. One in the same or all in one?

Rage.

Revelation.

Innocence lost.

She was lost. Numb. Uncertain. Demoralized. Her sense of self—as fragile as it already was—was crumbling like mortar crumbling between old bricks. She was fading fast. Murky tendrils rose from the depths to ensnare her. And they did. She felt it encircle her like a coiling snake and cover her mind, bind her with its inky blot of threatening, all-consuming existence. Too much for her mind to comprehend, too unbelievable for her soul to accept. Too much for her heart to bear.

She went under.

****

"And the psychics?"

The self-styled emissary was furious. A quiet storm with the promise of untold destruction waited in the gathering clouds behind his coal-black eyes. The harsh glare from the fluorescent lights overhead gleamed off his bald head. His impressive six-foot-five-inch frame was draped in an expensive suit, tailored in shades of gray and black. It contrasted nicely with his terra cotta complexion. His face was flushed, a vein throbbing in his forehead. He sat at his desk and looked up at his personal aide, Emmanuel Snow.

Emmanuel's face was impassive, but his employer knew better. He knew to look behind the cracks, beyond the uncertainty in his eyes. He knew that Emmanuel feared him, as he should. The news Emmanuel had brought him was unacceptable.

"They are in recovery, sir," Emmanuel replied, hands clasped before him. His boss could see Emmanuel willing himself not to shift uncomfortably, although it took all his power not to do so. Instead, a nerve twitched near his left eye. "They were instructed to possess our expendables on the scene. Detective Regan and Sergeant Avis. However, they were still weak from her previous manifestation. So—"

"So, you sent them into the field anyway?" the emissary interjected. "You knew they weren't ready for her, even in her weakened state."

"I thought I could handle it, sir," Emmanuel replied, his voice strained.

"Clearly, you could not," the emissary said, rising from his seat. He buttoned the jacket of his three-piece designer suit. "What is their status now?"

Emmanuel did not have to refer to his tablet for an update. "Stable, sir. All seven are immersed in a liquid sedative solution bath to repair their damaged synapses. Then we will begin the process of strengthening their shared links to heal the hive mind."

Out of commission. Forecasting of the divine sort was stalled for the moment. They would have to settle for more traditional, more humane ways of conducting business. It meant a return to a more hands-on approach. Old-fashioned threats and bribes for the politicians in their pocket. Quarterly reports would have to be ascertained by legal and less-divine ways. In short, it meant the emissary would have to do more himself. A vein in his forehead throbbed at the thought.

"You realize how your ineptitude has jeopardized our company?" he bellowed, smashing a fist onto his desk. "The sisters are some of our most valuable assets. They must be protected and utilized delicately!"

"I realize that, sir. I . . . I miscalculated," Emmanuel replied. "In my zest to procure the vessel, I endangered the sisters. I am sorry, sir."

"Bah."

The emissary walked around his desk and paused in front of Emmanuel. A light sheen of sweat coated the younger man's face. His throat moved as he swallowed, as if doing his best to stop himself from running out the room. The emissary took a step closer. "You do know who I am, correct?"

"Y-you are the emissary, sir," Emmanuel said, despite his dry mouth.

"My true name."

"Moradi. Amir Moradi, sir."

"Yes, that is right—Amir Moradi, CEO of MalGenPro Labs. I am the emissary, the chosen one. Not you. Me. You will do well to remember that."

"Yes . . . sir." Emmanuel said, using every bit of willpower to wring the trickle of agitation out of his voice.

Suddenly, the light seemed to drain from the room, and the shadows thickened. The emissary appeared . . . different. Bigger. More imposing. Severe. As if he had drawn the darkness into himself. For a moment between heartbeats, there was no white in his eyes, only unrelenting blackness. Tension neared critical mass. Oxygen became a luxury. Survival a necessity.

Against his will, Emmanuel took a step back, regretting the move instantly. In the blink of an eye, the room returned to normal. Moradi appeared to be his regular self, and the sun's rays seemed welcome once more. Emmanuel released a breath he did realize he had been holding. "Was there anything else, sir?" he wheezed.

"Haven't you done enough?" Moradi sneered. "Clearly, I will have to take matters into my own hands. Wait, what about the Cairns police department? Where are we with that?"

"Scorched earth, sir."

"Excellent."

Mortals were not ready for those who were empowered. In the few instances of a revealing, when one with special abilities publicly displayed his or her powers, the emissary used his vast power and connections to "sanitize" the site. So far, there had been minor incidents from the low-level ones. But with her? Scorched earth. No survivors meant no police reports or sensational talks with the press.

"And where is she now? Were the psychics able to track her once she opened the water portal?"

Emmanuel averted his gaze briefly before forcing himself to look back at his superior. "No, sir. They were still recovering when the vessel and Cyrus vanished."

Cyrus. That was still beyond mind boggling. Moradi shook his head. The mission had not changed. He still needed them both, but now it was harder to pinpoint them. They were momentarily blinded. And yet . . .

"Your contact? The fixer?"

"Ariadne?"

"Yes. Fly her in from Italy. We have further use of her unique skills."

"Why, yes, sir."

****

"Cyrus?"

"Yeah?"

"At what point do we like, I dunno, take her to a hospital?"

Cyrus and Ramona looked down at the mysterious dark-skinned woman's troubled, sleeping form. With the grace of a higher power, or maybe sheer, dumb luck, they had been able to transport her from the cramped bookstore to Ramona's studio, a few minutes away, by way of her ghastly yet cheerful hearse. Of course, by that point, the woman was semi-conscious and talking to herself. Incoherent muttering and startling gasps or mournful sobs.

They wanted desperately to help her. Ramona kept turning around to check on them both as she expertly navigated through San Francisco traffic. Cyrus held the nameless woman close, head buried in her massive dark locks, murmuring reassurances to her in his deep New York accent. Ramona felt a lump in her throat. Whatever they had been through in the last twenty-four hours had bonded the two survivors. She could not help but feel a twinge of jealousy.

With as much care as they could muster, and yet still get her from point A to point B post haste, Cyrus and Ramona ushered the woman into Ramona's small apartment. At that point, the nameless woman slipped into unconsciousness. Whatever she was dealing with internally scared the other two. They sat on either side of her in Ramona's bed, the woman swathed in unicorn bedding.

"She doesn't have any identification," Cyrus said absentmindedly, dabbing her forehead with a damp cloth. His eyes narrowed in concentration. "We experienced that scenario already. Wasn't fun. Trust me."

"But still . . ." Ramona sighed and crossed her arms, her bangles and bracelets clicking. "I really didn't mean for her to wig out after I told her about the tattoo. Nothin's been proven though!" She threw up her hands.

Cyrus looked up. "No, it's not your fault. It's just been a very draining and emotional few hours for us. Yesterday, I was shrimping in Australia. Now I'm in San Francisco in a stranger's house tending to another stranger with magical powers."

Despite the dire situation, Ramona's eyes twinkled. "For real? It must have been pretty epic."

Cyrus chuckled and nodded. "It was. Though, when I thought for sure I was going to die, it was scary and weird seeing her controlling water. But now, just thinking about it, it was pretty bad ass. She's like a superhero."

"Definitely," Ramona said, nodding as she stared at the mystery woman. "I wish I could have seen it."

Cyrus looked down at the woman and sighed. "Well, they pop up whenever we're threatened. I seriously don't want to be threatened again."

"I can *totally* get behind that," the punk Asian girl replied.

"But knowing our luck, we may get a chance to see her powers again."

They returned their full attention as the woman continued to react to whatever was playing behind her eyes.

****

Falling.

She sank deeper, as if a steel ball was chained around her ankle, pulling her to the ocean floor, which was littered with shards of shattered lives. Beams of light, cold and bright, cut through, trying to probe the bottom but never quite reaching before darkness sent it scurrying back.

Innocence lost? Had she ever been truly innocent? The innocent were not damned forever.

Maybe I should just kill myself. End it all now before I hurt people. Before I hurt Ramona and Cyrus.

She felt something dark and furtive shift deep in her core. Was it responding to her suicidal thoughts? Did whoever or whatever it was know she feared it?

This doorway in my soul that leads to me doing . . . crazy things is not normal. It brings only destruction.

She thought about the wake of destruction she had left behind. The police station. The hospital. When she lost control, others suffered. She could not allow that to happen. Not to her newfound friends.

She would kill herself first.

A girl ran. Her bare feet pounded the hard-packed dirt. The warm African breeze swept back her glorious mane of hair. Her bracelets clinked as she pushed back towering blades of grass. Her heart thundered in her chest. Excitement thrilled throughout her panting body. He was behind her, as silent as any predator after dark. An ominous presence, feeling given form.

And she was his prey.

She ran. In that moment, she heard labored breathing behind her. Faint and controlled but still audible. He was gaining ground. She leapt over a puddle. She heard him splash into it. Feeling cocky, she glanced back. To her surprise, no one was there. Her momentary confusion was all her pursuer needed. He ambushed her from the side.

The air was crushed from her lungs upon impact, her vision fractured into shards of black and red. They tumbled through the blades of grass. She struggled, but he was too strong. The young teenager, no more than fourteen years old, the same age as her, pinned her down and held her wrists to the ground. He grinned fiercely at her, breathing hard. "I win. Again!"

She focused on her controlling her breathing, struggling feebly in his vise-like grip. Annoyed, she looked him in the eye. "You cheated."

Laughing, he rose from the ground and offered his hand. "Never. I'm just better at this than you."

She stared at his hand, sighed, and then clasped it. "I suppose. I was better this time though. I almost lost you."

His laughter shifted to a soft chuckle. "Almost. But I will always find you."

A fantasy? A memory?

It felt like one and yet . . . her mind would not accept it.

She continued her downward spiral to the vast nothingness of non-existence, of non-corporeal purgatory. It grew darker the lower she descended. Fewer bubbles in the unimaginable fathoms below.

Suddenly, the tattoo on her chest started to glow faintly. She felt it stretch its tingling fingers throughout her cold body. She was willing herself to die. The mysterious tattoo was willing her to live.

Dead parts were reawakened. Numb nerves stung with creeping life. Still she fought against her survival instincts. Something scratched at the veil of her mind from inside. Something that would not be ignored. It was survival, and it spoke to her by dredging up a warning issued a short time ago.

"Try to remember. Only then will you be truly prepared. And then, when it all falls, you must choose."

What did that mean? she wondered, frustrated. Then pinpricks of realization broke up the mist of forgetfulness. Those disjointed glimpses into the lives of other women were somehow tied to her. She had to prepare herself. She would have to stop fighting herself first.

"You must choose."

Choose life, not death.

"I choose them. I choose Cyrus and Ramona. I choose . . . me." She embraced herself. The tattoo flared brighter, the phoenix lifted its beak higher, spread its wings farther. She thought she heard a trill of awakening in her soul. It was reknitting itself together, reclaiming pieces long thought lost to the firmament of a place neither here nor there.

"Nothing is as it seems."

"No, it's not. I am not some dark, malevolent thing," she said to no one in particular as bands of water coruscated around her in foamy bubbles. It restored, replenished, and renewed. *I am so much more. I am . . . more.*

She was a vessel of great power. Mysterious and as old as time. Like her. A woman with many names, many faces. It was time to integrate them all. Time to reclaim her new life. It was time.

****

"Do you think she'll be okay?" Cyrus asked, reluctant to leave her side.

"I think so," Ramona replied after withdrawing a Blow Pop from her mouth. She licked her lips and then pushed up her glasses. "I mean, she's only sleeping now. Finally."

Cyrus returned his gaze to the woman. He took in her smooth skin, which reminded him of dark chocolate flowing over an athletic body, strong but not too muscular, feminine but capable. The glorious banner of her tumbling natural locks nearly obscured the pillow upon which her head rested. Her eyelids no longer flickered or fluttered, caught in an REM battle only she could see and fight. She seemed at peace. She looked so innocent and yet so powerful. Power radiated from her, but why did she remain asleep? How could she be so lost? Cyrus tried to suppress the uncomfortable feeling in the pit of his stomach. In that moment, caught up in her majestic beauty amidst Ramona's preadolescent bed sheets, a throwback to 1980s cartoons, Cyrus knew he would die protecting her. They had bonded. If he could reach in and pull her out, he would have.

I wish I could find you, he thought. His fingers brushed her hand as her index fingers twitched. *What's going on in your head? How can I reach you?*

"I don't know," he said finally. "She may need us."

"We'll only be the next room, Romeo," Ramona teased, her

lousy attempt to lighten the mood.

Cyrus's eyes widened, and then he stood up. "It's not like that!"

A mischievous grin spread across the petite Asian woman's face. "The way you just sprang to your feet says otherwise."

He felt his cheeks grow warm. "You don't know anything."

"Methinks he doth protest too much."

Cyrus let out a frustrated growl.

"Okay, okay, come on, ya big baby." Ramona threw up her hands in defeat. "We'll only be in the next room. Let's eat some of that Goodie Box stuff."

Reluctantly, Cyrus followed her out of the room, compelled by his grumbling stomach.

He took in his new surroundings for the first time since arriving. Ramona lived in a small studio that looked just like the Writers' Block. Clothes were tossed over a patchwork couch. Venetian blinds were pulled up in front of a casement window that overlooked a busy street. It appeared as if the walls themselves had thrown up piles of books. Ramona's abode smelled of old paper, scented candles, and the faint aroma of coffee. He felt the stiffness leave his shoulders. It seemed like a safe place. He paused at a bookshelf before making his way to the breakfast nook. Maybe things would all work out after all.

"Can I ask you a question?"

"You just did."

"What?"

"Never mind. Shoot."

Cyrus sat in a chair near the pub table. "How are you able to afford all this? You're living in San Francisco, of all places. It's one of the most expensive cities in the country."

Ramona hummed as she placed dinnerware on the table. She looked up as she set his hamburger on a plate. "My grandmother died. She left me some money. Drove my father crazy. He thought that no woman should be in charge of her finances. It's supposedly the man's job."

Cyrus knotted his brow. "Sorry, but that's stupid."

Ramona shrugged. "Well, Father is old school. Anyway, I

was already going to SFAI, and I love it here. So, after my grandmother died, I bought a book café that was going out of business. I can afford the rent here now." She laughed.

Cyrus nodded before taking a big bite of his hamburger. Grease dribbled down his chin. He wiped it with a napkin. "This really is good."

"Goodie Box and all," Ramona reminded him, taking a sip from her chocolate milkshake. "So, what about you, Mr. Supermodel? Where are you from? You have that trademark east coast accent. Manhattan? Brooklyn? "

Cyrus swallowed his food, already dreading where the conversation was headed. "Actually, I'm from Queens. But my parents moved from Afghanistan to the States when my mom was pregnant with me."

Ramona titled her head to the side like a bird.

It was harder to swallow the next bite. In fact, he lost his appetite altogether. "Can we talk about something else?"

"Sure thing, boss," Ramona replied, obviously curious but respectful not to pry.

An uncomfortable silence stretched between them. Then Cyrus rose from his seat and looked toward the bedroom. "I should check . . ." His voice trailed off as he stuffed his hands in his pockets, took them out, then put them back in. "I wish I had a cigarette."

Ramona arched one eyebrow. "You smoke?"

Cyrus grunted and shrugged. "Yes. No. I dunno. I quit a few months ago, but for the last couple of hours, I've been itching for a drag." A hopeful look crossed his face. "Do you have any cigarettes?"

Ramona gave him a long blink that dripped of boredom. "I have other vices." She gestured to her books.

"Touché." Cyrus would have to go the convenience store then. His body was craving nicotine. "Why didn't I want a cigarette until now? It's probably because this was the longest time we haven't been attacked."

"Plus, Goodie Box."

"Yup, can't forget Goodie Box."

The atmosphere in the studio changed. Akin to the sky changing from dusk to dawn or vice versa. One could see it gradually, but to behold the metamorphosis second by second was impossible. The closest sensation was that of pressure lifted from burdened limbs. They looked at each other. Her! They rushed to the room and pushed open the door.

She stood by the window, her profile facing them. Horizontal slats of sunlight filtered into the room, silhouetting her. She wore a loose-fitting, off-the-shoulder blouse over a pair of leggings. In the dim light, her tattoo pulsed in rhythm to the rise and fall of her chest. Then, ever so slowly, the mysterious woman turned toward them. A slow smile broke across her face, like the return of the long-forgotten sun in the realm of eternal darkness.

"I remember!"

11

"We started it all. We were the first tribe, and soon we will be dust. But not you."

"I don't understand, High One," the old man's blue-eyed, dark-skinned pupil replied. Fear took root in her eyes. "What's wrong with our people?"

He sat before her, all dust and bones and smelling of time itself; parchments, dyes, and creeping death. His midnight skin was covered in a fine white powder that settled over the cracks in his weathered flesh. Tall and long-limbed, he was the shaman to his people. He was powerful beyond belief, since he was a frequent visitor to other realms and was well-versed in the mystic arts. He prayed it would be enough. Perhaps his prayers would be answered now?

"We are dying. Before the next half-moon, our tribe will be stricken with a great disease. I have seen the portents and omens in the stars. The Wandering Children will wander no more."

"Are you sure?" Alarm made her voice come out strained.

The old man nodded soberly. He had checked, double-checked, and even triple-checked, but the results all led to the same conclusion: the decimation of their people. "Would I lie about this?"

She shifted uncomfortably and lowered her gaze. "No, most revered one. Can anything be done? Can I help?"

A sad smile tugged at his dry lips. Always willing to help. She was the best of them. She had a huge heart and a spirit that was infectious with its goodwill and love for her family and fellow tribesmen. Tumbling locks framed her lovely face, the color of dark chocolate. Her pale eyes contrasted exotically with her complexion. It marked her as different. Athletic. Fleet footed.

The only thing that could possibly surpass her athletic prowess was the size of her heart. He often saw her singing to the children or helping the old mothers with basket weaving and cooking. Sometimes she would sneak off to hunt game with the boys, much to her chieftain father's chagrin.

"You are the best of us. I have watched since you were born. I knew you were special from the moment you drew your first breath and your mother drew her last. The gods saw fit to gift us with you as they accepted your blessed mother into their embrace. You will continue our teachings and embody our will."

Excitement tempered by anxiety flowed through her. It was such an honor to be chosen by the shaman, and yet she could hardly suppress her mounting fear. The words rushed out of her mouth before common sense could register. "But I'm not worthy! What about him?"

She pointed to the illustration of a warrior painted on the cavern wall. Memories, new and old, quivered like a water bead on the tip of a trembling leaf. It dropped as she thought of her oldest friend. He was the only boy to welcome her on hunts, the only one to accept her as an equal. He had laughing eyes. He still had the boyish charms and visage, but he was grown now, like her. She had watched him grow up from a skinny boy playing pranks and competing with his brothers to a strong warrior, whom men wanted to follow into battle and women wanted to marry. Always with the laughing eyes. Her old friend.

"No," was all the shaman said at first, hardness strengthening his jaw, clenched teeth adding to his resolve. "He is not worthy. If I simply wanted a warrior, I would have chosen him to be the vessel. But I do not. I require . . . more. I require you."

"But what can I do? I'm just me," she said. She was quick to offer assistance without knowing what it would entail. She hated herself for showing weakness and doubt.

"That is all I require, child. You are a rare bird capable of singing our song until the end of time. Your song is for the ages, my little sparrow."

He rose to his feet. She followed suit.

"I am still seeking the right enchantment to preserve your spirit." He smiled as he lifted her chin with his long fingers. "Do not fear, girl. It is not the end. Only the beginning."

A lump rose in her throat and prevented words from coming out right away. "Yes, High One. But is there truly nothing we can do for our tribe?"

He removed his hand. "I am doing what I can. I am not a god, you know. Silly girl." He waved his hand dismissively. "Now go. Speak of this to no one."

Reluctantly, she bowed her head and exited the cave, only to run into her old childhood friend. How long had he been lurking there? Had he heard what was said? It was dusk, and the shadows played across his face, obscuring his features. Sweat glistened on his broad chest like dew in the morning. Her eyes alighted upon the lion-tooth necklace around his neck. His first kill, his pride and joy. His arms were adorned with tribal bands and trinkets. His breathing was still labored from a successful hunt. He held a hare by its ears.

"Oh! You startled me. What are you doing here?" she breathed out in a string of words that seemed to blend together.

His handsome face regarded her for a moment in silence. His full lips were pursed, and his high cheeks glistened with sweat. His eyes did not laugh as his lips pulled back into a smile. "I could ask you the same question, my friend. But I was hunting. I found something."

She forced a smile as she gazed at the dead rabbit. "Indeed, you have! You are so strong and brave. You will make a fine husband one day."

He smirked. "Is that so? You wish to be my wife?"

She elbowed him playfully and headed away from the cave entrance. "There you go again. Must you always chase?"

"If I must," he said as she walked away. "You cannot shake me or lose me. I will always find you."

****

The days leading up to the sickness were the hardest she had ever endured. To bear the secret kept her stomach perpetually in knots. She wanted so desperately to share it, to ease the burden that weighed on her soul. Her fellow tribespeople knew something was different about her, but they respected her privacy, and she kept her distance.

She treasured each second in its own way. Her people, her brothers and sisters of the plains, children of the veld, were truly special. Always on the move. Highly intelligent, they had their own culture, language, and way of life. A way of life that was about to die.

"But not forever," she found herself saying, arms crossed, as she walked along a well-worn path and the wind stirred her hair. "I've been chosen to keep our way of life alive. But will it matter if all my friends and family die? And the children . . ." A sob escaped her, followed by hot, salty tears.

"Why are you crying?"

She froze. Mentally kicking herself, she spun around in the gloom to see the warrior. Concern tightened his features. She wanted to flee as he closed the distance between them. He reached for her. Sparks ignited beneath her skin when he lightly held her forearms.

"Am I not allowed to be sad?" she asked. "Must I always be cheerful and happy for the sake of the tribe?"

"No."

He drew her closer to him. She felt a new tension in the air. The night animals began to cry out to each other.

"You know you can tell me anything," he said. "Are we not friends?"

"Yes," she replied, trying to will the tightness from her body. Any other female from their tribe would have dreamed of such a moment, but all she dreamed of was fleeing. "Really, I'm fine."

He lifted her chin with his hand and stared into her eyes. "No, you're not. I'm going to ask you a very important question, and I think you already know what it is."

She did. She tried to turn her head, but he kept a firm grasp on her chin. "Please don't. I can't—"

"I must. Be my wife."

She broke away as tears continued their trek down her chin. She did not need this. Not today. "Why must you ruin this? Why ruin our friendship?"

His nostrils flared. Anger and indignation puffed out his chest. He balled his hands into fists. "*Ruin our friendship?* I'm trying to take it to the next level, to unify us. Don't think for one second some other woman will not want my hand in marriage!"

"Then ask one of them! I don't want to marry you," she seethed, the words spewing from her lips. "You're my friend. Why can't that be enough?"

"It's never been enough," he fumed. "I wanted your love, but now . . . now I don't want anything from you."

"Please, just—"

He waved her off. She stepped toward him, but the look he gave her chilled the blood in her veins.

"I should thank you," he said. "You just made my choice very easy."

Then he was gone. And she was left there, hugging herself once again, her tears still mourning the loss of life, as she knew it.

****

The hut smelled of dinner. Flat cakes cooking filled the home of the chieftain and his daughter, who had a secret. Normally, mealtimes were overripe with nonstop talking and overflowing with laughter. It was a joyous time for family to connect and to recount their day. Conversations ranged from the birth of a calf to the glorious hunt of a gazelle. The chieftain knew much of this before his excited daughter shared what she learned that day. Still, he encouraged her to tell him. He would not dim that beautiful light in her eyes, which were the color of the sky. That night was different though. That night, she was oddly silent.

"Daughter, what troubles you?"

She looked up from the hot ashes and glowing coals over

which she was preparing their meal and wiped the sweat from her forehead with the back of her hand. "Father, I am well. The bread is almost ready."

Like the shaman, the chieftain was tall. He was also sinewy and muscular, especially for a man in his later years. He had a strong, stern face and eyes that brimmed with wisdom. The chieftain was regal and wise with a kind heart and a disposition toward tough love. As an expert hunter, he was conditioned to see the unseen, so, his daughter's apparent duress did not go unnoticed.

"What ails you?"

Silence.

He rose to his feet and approached his only child, who reminded him so much of his deceased wife. He sighed. Why pretend? Why waste time with questions to which he already knew the answer? "A great honor will be bestowed upon you. You will ensure our legacy lives on."

She blinked at him. "You . . . you know?"

Nodding, he held her gaze. "I knew before you did. The old man told me first. He believes with his heart of hearts that you are the vessel for our tribe's legacy. A daughter of eternity. Life personified."

"But, Father, why didn't you tell me?" Hurt and disbelief clouded her eyes.

The chieftain shrugged. "I suppose I needed to come to grips with it myself. As chieftain, I believe the shaman wholeheartedly. This will ensure our survival. As a father, my heart breaks over and over."

Ugly gut-wrenching sobs burst from her lips as she embraced the man who shared her blood and was responsible for the woman she had become. She let all her trepidation, frustration, and fear flow from her eyes as she pressed her face against her father's strong chest. She would never know, but silent, stoic tears betrayed the leader of their people. Life, as they knew it, was ending. There was only brief, fleeting sanctuary in her father's strong arms.

"You are life, daughter. We are death."

****

She thought I did not hear her in the shaman's cave, the spurned warrior mused as he sharpened his knife. *I had just finished my hunt when I saw her dart into the cave. I was curious, so I followed, but I kept my distance. I clung to the many shadows his cold, dank home afforded me. I heard it all.*

A slow headache throbbed from his clenched jaw. The crackling glow of the fire pit made his bloodshot eyes appear demonic, full of murderous rage. To be ignored by the one he had always loved and wanted since childhood. Was it all a game to her?

I can understand the sway of her charm. Her beauty and smile are enough to drive any man insane. But she is still a woman. Unworthy of the task given her. I am the best man to save our people. I am the strongest. And if she will not be my wife, she will not be the vessel.

The flickering flames cast their enchanting light on his instrument of death. His eyes no longer laughed. In fact, they would never laugh again. They saw only her, the love that would never be, covered in the blood for which she was responsible. Drowned in the blood that would be hers and hers alone.

Even when she lied to me—to my face!—I gave no indication that I knew. I knew she had been chosen and not me. Even she seemed surprised. I would have forgiven her that if she had not denied my all-consuming love for her. My task is clear. I know what I must do.

The rock sent a spray of sparks off his gleaming blade. He ached to bury it deep inside her soft, wet flesh, to feel it tear through muscle and puncture her organs.

He rose to his feet, his face resolute. "Our tribe will live on through me."

****

One day, the great sickness struck. It flowed over the Wandering Children and stopped them in their tracks, bringing them to their knees, coughing and choking and spewing the blood and gore that once stewed in their stomachs. Great wracking sobs, bone-shuddering tremors, and wails of the desperate consumed the once-great people. Many were felled in the first three days. It was calamity in its purest, most undiluted sense. The elders did what they could to ease their people's suffering, but it was no use. Mothers cried out in hoarse whispers as their dead children were pulled from their lesioned arms.

One by one, they succumbed to the lethal illness. Even the livestock. With grim horror, those who were not afflicted watched as loved ones withered like grapes on a vine. Mothers wept for children who were beyond their care in this world. Children hollered for mothers who would never hold them again. Death had come for them all.

The old man watched as well. From his cavern, he watched and prepared the rites that would keep his prize pupil immortal. He had not slept for days and had eaten little. For what seemed like an eternity, he sat still, his body made misty and at times incorporeal by the fumes of burning potpourri and smoky incense. Flakes from his powdery face paint floated down from his prone form whenever a cold draft whispered through his dank, chilly abode. He did not feel it. Eyes rolled to reveal milky whites, the shaman was plucking the secrets from the universe. He envisioned that, using his hand, he could scoop stars from the firmament and squeeze their life into cups of liquid silver and platinum. They had burned for countless ages, so perhaps their longevity could be shared.

The chieftain was no exception to the disease. The sickness sat warm and happy in his chest, twisting him from the inside out. His proud bearing was reduced to a phlegm-spitting, shaking form, his servants dabbing him constantly with wet cloths.

He had forbidden his daughter to enter his domicile and see him in such a state. So, she spent most of her time alone. Curiously, her headstrong warrior friend from her childhood was nowhere to be seen. He had been expected back from a hunt the day before the great sickness descended.

I chose wisely, the old man thought sourly. *We need someone dependable, not someone more interested in game instead of the fate of his people. The girl will keep us alive—after a fashion.* He smiled at the thought. It was his only consolation.

On the twelfth day, he summoned her. The silent stars had aligned. The mystical properties were at their zenith. It was a night of magic and rebirth. It was also a night of death. Only a third of the tribe still lived, and only a fraction of those were still healthy. That included his pupil. She remained unblemished and unspoiled by the ravages of disease. Even the shaman counted himself among the number of those afflicted. It mattered little to him now. All that mattered was the ceremony. Their survival.

She trembled slightly as she walked, realization weighing like stones on her shoulders. The shaman rested heavily on his staff, sweating profusely, beckoning her with his blistered, pus-pocked hand. The somber beat of drums floated mournfully in the air. Flowers flanked her path to the stone altar erected in the heart of the village. Some sobbed. Others looked on dully with cloudy, sightless eyes. A small child, half his face covered in dripping boils, pointed numbly to his salvation. She caught his eye with her tear-filled gaze. She stopped and cast a furtive glance at the shaman.

"Come, girl," he whispered in a tone like crackling leaves caught in a stiff, odorous wind blowing from the underworld. "Life will not wait. Answer its call."

She took a deep breath, lifted her chin higher, and continued forward. Each step seemed to charge the air with raw, unexplainable magic. Her resolve strengthened the bonds, washing away her doubt. Her determination to save her people was the only thing that kept her moving toward the altar.

The old man joined her. "Look upon our vessel, my people," he began, presenting the nervous girl to the remnants of their once-proud tribe. "We were the first to migrate. The first to leave our place of birth and explore a world we knew nothing about. We headed west. Our gods saw fit to grant us safe passage during those early days. They came with us. They spoke to us. They made us richer in ways we never dreamed possible. Our blessed Yoruba, we still thank you for all you have given us. Please guide our hand in steering our chosen one, our vessel, to embody our teachings, our values, and wisdom until the end of days!"

The remaining tribespeople cheered and praised their heavenly deities for the last time. Hope glittered in their failing eyes, powered their hearts, which beat slower with each passing moment. They were beginning to see why this was necessary.

"After many days of fasting and praying during the greatest tragedy to befall our people, I have prepared a ceremony to infuse her with our essence, our spirit. Long after we are dust, she will remain young and beautiful. She will never die. She will carry our message of love and unity until the end of days. She will remain our favored daughter for eternity."

He gestured for his aides to bring the ailing chieftain closer. The dying leader of a decimated people shook violently as he approached his daughter. He kept a respectful, stoic distance, which upset her, but he did not wish to infect her. "My children, we can rest easy now," he said. "Change has never frightened us. We have always adapted. Death will be no different. We will accept this and will die happily knowing my only child, the very best of us, will endure the passages of time. Daughter?" He indicated the altar.

The girl, the vessel, hesitantly turned away from her mentors, one of blood and one of magic, and gingerly lay on the stone altar. Candles burned. Incense wafted into her nostrils. The old man approached her and held her arm. With ink-dipped fingertips, he traced a symbol that rose into a bird. He stopped tracing as he reached the side of her throat where her jaw and neck began. "Lay down and cross your arms."

As she crossed her arms across her chest, she saw the markings of the tattoo realign itself into something stylized and beautiful. Tribal and teeming with hidden power. It made her skin pulse with power. Curling mists enshrouded her, obscuring her vision. She felt airborne, buoyed by the winds of the impossible. Then a sharp sweet pain ripped through her.

She gasped, moaned in fearful delight, greedily sucking in air. Each cell seemed to burst from an intense pressure mixed with pleasure. Her skin melted in a million pinpricks that seemed to . . . sing to her. Her soul sighed. She cried out and reached for her father, who had become a misty apparition a few feet in front of her. He might as well have been miles away.

"It begins."

She felt herself lift higher. Clouds brushed against her ears. Her mass of dark curls became weightless. Power coursed through her. Magic in its purest form became acquainted with every cell and knew her in ways she never dreamed possible. There was nowhere to hide when her own body was being invaded. It whispered to her, and she heard her soul reply. It spoke in a language not even the shaman knew. Only her. The magic, wild and yet in control, told her what it would do. Her body would become an ageless temple impervious to the effects of aging and disease. She could only part her lips in wonder as she felt her soul become something new, more durable. Timeless.

She was becoming immortal.

Thoughts could not form coherently. Sensations rolled through her and undulated in waves of life-preserving enchantment. Higher still she rose. She felt herself righted as her arms uncrossed and floated at her sides. Coils and bands of indescribable colors twisted around her. A smile formed on her lips. Her resistance ebbed, and for the first time, she began to accept this final task, this last mission bestowed upon her by her people. She would honor them and spread their teachings, their gifts, and their insights to the world. She was excited for the changes to come.

Shouting.

Her eyes snapped opened.

It was hard to orient herself, but through the mists of smoke and magic, she saw red. Splashes of it. She cried out in horror as she bore witness to a murderous group of tribesmen cutting through the survivors like a scythe through wheat.

Her father's guards tried to protect him, but they were no match for the invaders' bloodthirsty leader. He advanced upon her dying father with eyes that were familiar despite the insanity that had possessed them. It was her childhood friend!

He raised his bloody knife high. She banged against the invisible force field that kept her rooted to the altar. The blade might as well have plunged into her own heart as it tore into her father's. He did not cry out as he dropped to one knee, bathed in a torrent of his own blood. There was no fight left in the once-great chieftain. She howled her grief.

The old man was next.

"You should have chosen me!" the insane warrior bellowed as he kicked the old man's staff away. The shaman fell to the blood-soaked ground. She heard something snap.

"Do you not see it?" the warrior cried. "I am great and powerful. Admit you were wrong!"

The shaman looked up. It took all his strength. Defiance still burned like hot coals in pale eyes. He sneered. "I admit nothing. You proved me right. And we both know this is not about being selected as the vessel."

They both turned to the one who meant so much to them, frozen in a bath of magical properties. Her outrage and grief was palpable despite the barriers. The warrior's face softened a little. Her blue eyes were his undoing. They had driven him mad. There was no turning back now. And if he could not have her…

His blade flashed once more. A spray of blood erupted from the shaman's throat. A smile animated his lips as the dirt soaked up the last of his life. Then the warrior advanced toward her.

Each step sounded her imminent demise. He kept his eyes fixed on hers, his handsome face a quagmire of rage, insanity, and determination. His eyes laughed at a cruel, malicious joke that kept him resolute on his deadly purpose.

Her heart pounded against her chest like a caged animal. She wished she could be free too. The cries of the massacre drifted back to her on poisoned winds. Then she and the warrior were face to face.

"Why?"

His hand gripped the blade tighter. Scorn, thick and hot, pulsated from his tense form. "Am I worthy now?"

Puzzlement flashed in her grief-stricken eyes. "What?"

He grinned ferociously. Up close, she could see the splatter of their people's blood mixed with bits of flesh on his face. "Am I worthy now to have you as my wife? Have I proven myself worthy of your love?"

Madness.

She saw it not for what it was. An insecure, weak-spirited monster. Proud and arrogant. Strong but misplaced, without leadership qualities. Lustful, incapable of love. How could he ever lead their people? How could he ever be entrusted with their legacy?

"You never were. Not in the way you wanted. But now this . . ." She gestured to the fading remnants of their people. Her dead father and her mentor, the shaman. "I could never love a monster like you. Yes, you are unworthy."

Tears mixed in with the blood. His strong jaw trembled slightly. He bowed, nodding softly. Lifting his head, he regarded her with a sad smile. "Well, no more running. You can't shake me this time. I've got you. "

She tried to recoil from the blade that caught the glint of the hot angry sun, but he was too fast. Much to her surprise, the blade passed through the barriers the magic had erected as it was changing her body. How did it get through? Enchanted? By whom?

Cold obsidian bit into the taut flesh of her abdomen. She felt it tear through muscle and slice through organs. The pain was excruciating. She slid to her knees clutching the gory ruin of her stomach. She looked up at him in shock. Her lips parted to say something, but only blood poured out.

He looked down at her, a towering sentinel craving the taste of human blood.

Her vision blurred. Blood continue to flow like a bubbling brook from the fatal wound. Would the magic fail her? Were they doomed?

Her body was dying. She felt her heart slow with each beat. A chill stole through her body, from her core to her limbs. She slumped to the side. Blood soaked her tunic and stained the stone slab, spilling off the edges. With a detachment only the dying could feel, she watched it splatter the dirt below. It was getting harder to keep her eyes open. Her tribe's death throes were no longer a deafening roar but a whimpering static that grew quieter by the second. She wished she could die at her father's side. He would rot in the sun. She would, too, if she could help it.

The warrior watched her die in the space between heartbeats. His breathing had slowed down. His head tilted, he watched the imagined love of his life fade away. Then he turned his back and walked off. When she died, he would gather the rest of his brothers and move on. They were the Wandering Children, were they not?

He stopped and turned around, eager for one last sight.

His eyes widened.

She was airborne.

She looked down upon her dead, bloody body. How was it possible? The warrior seemed just as surprised. She looked at her arms and her legs and cried out. They were insubstantial and glowing. The tattoo on her chest flared to life, starting at the symbol and then up to the great bird that flew up her arm and across her throat. In her soul, she felt it trill a death-defying shriek. Her soul had become untethered from her body. But this was not how it was supposed to be! She pulsed with colors that would never have names. She felt sensations that no human could feel. She was a specter in a class by herself, no longer bound to the mortal coil.

Screaming out a war cry, the warrior threw his blade at her. It sailed right through her as she began to disperse. He rushed the stone altar that still teemed with wild, untamed magic. By the time he reached it, she was no more. Only the body that was meant to live until the end of time lay there, rotting in the sun.

12

"So, what happened next?" Ramona's eyes were wide behind her big black-framed glasses, so caught up in the story she had forgotten to breathe. She took a deep gulp of air and then looked around for her milkshake. Realizing not much was left, she shook it irritably and then placed it back on the floor beside her.

Cyrus's mouth opened in shock. He closed it and rubbed his forehead, dazed. "I may start smoking again. Seriously."

The nameless woman chuckled softly to herself, perched on the edge of the bed, hands clasped over her knee. It was odd to recall those memories with such clarity. Her emotions ran hot and thick. She recalled her father and the pride in his eyes whenever they interacted. He was a good man, a great leader, and an even better father. Her eyes burned as a lump stretched in her throat. The chieftain was but dust and bones now, forgotten in the winds of time. But not entirely. She remembered. She remembered it all.

"Excuse me . . ." A fat tear rolled down her cheek. She laughed and dabbed at it with a knuckle. "I'm sorry. I haven't thought about that in such a long time. I recalled my father's face."

"Omigawd, sorry!" Ramona quickly got up and gave her a side hug. The immortal woman laughed. Cyrus even reached over and squeezed her hand. He did not say a word. The look on his face said it all. He was there for her. They both were.

She cared for Cyrus and Ramona as well. In the short time she had known them, they had developed an intense bond, a unity that transcended time and space. It linked her with the fisherman and the scribe. It was preordained. A shared destiny for them all. She placed her hand over his and leaned into Ramona's hug. It felt right after so long. If she could have stayed like that forever, she would have. But a story needed to be told and a battle won.

Clearing her throat, she released Cyrus's hand and withdrew from Ramona. She stood up and returned to the window, her back to them. Memories, good and bad, were returning to her, one by one. A random memory of her sipping soup with the old man in his cold cave swam to the surface. She smiled sadly. He was dead. He had died the day her warrior friend-turned-murderer butchered their surviving tribesmen. A thought pricked the back of her mind. Then how was the shaman still alive? Or was he? How was he able to still reach her infrequently?

"So, what happened next?" Ramona repeated, pushing up her glasses, childlike awe evident on her face. "What happened to that—what was his name? The betrayer dude."

The nameless woman was silent for a moment. "I don't know. I honestly don't."

"Wait, what? Seriously? Talk about anticlimactic!"

"Why do you say that?"

"You really don't know what happened to him?"

She knitted her brow in concentration. "All I remember is fading away. And he was there. So very angry."

Cyrus sat up straighter on the floor. "I think I get it now. Since that magical ceremony was interrupted, it couldn't finish the process. So, it only affected your spirit, right?" He rose, hands clasped, finally piecing things together. "But if the ritual wouldn't have been interrupted, you would have been truly immortal, mind, body, and—"

"Soul," she finished. Could that explain the gaps in her memory? The blind spots in her soul? Slowly, they were being filled in. She remembered being infused with the time-defying enchantment. The skin-tingling sensation as the wild magic altered her body to endure from that moment and beyond. Her friend with the eyes that used to laugh had tried to put a stop to it. He had succeeded only in killing her body. Yet she had endured. She was there. And he was dust. She did not try to stamp out the flame of satisfaction that thought kindled in her heart.

"But what about the names?"

"Names?"

"Didn't he have a name? Or you, for that matter?" Ramona inquired, drawing her knees to her chest. "Everybody has a name."

"We all start off with one, but maybe we don't always end up with one," the immortal woman replied vaguely, her tone surprisingly light and bereft of emotion. Her startling blue eyes were lost in a time warp of events spanning almost since the dawn of creation, seeing things in that moment that no one else could dream of. It would take some time to adjust. "I cannot recall his. Or mine. Lost in the winds of time, like so many things."

Once again, that nagging sensation. What was she missing? She was grateful for the slivers of memory returning to her, but something was still misplaced. Maybe she should have remembered those names. After all, names were power.

Silence.

Cyrus nodded. "Yup. Definitely going to start smoking again."

****

They needed a game plan, so they sat on Ramona's hardwood floor and came up with one. Ramona had brought binders of articles that were varying hues of yellow. They included sketches of random females. The common denominator was the unique tattoo emblazoned upon her arm whenever she used her powers.

She reached for one article with a blurry sketch of a woman. It looked to be set in Victorian England. Ramona cooed over her shoulder, a new lollipop lodged in her mouth. They both took in the soft features, complemented with a high bun. Her corset left her arms bare for the exception of decorative flowers bunched at the shoulders. Her corset flared out into a dress. She appeared lost despite her stoic, almost bland facial expression. The color of her dress was indistinguishable in the black-and-white photo, known only to the photographer and the mysterious woman.

Her eyes seemed alive on the page. Alluring even.

"Look," Ramona said, her face distorted by the lollipop grossly stretching out her left cheek. She made a loud sucking noise.

The nameless woman looked over at Ramona with a raised eyebrow. Sheepishly, the younger woman took a step back and removed the lollipop.

Returning to the old clipping, the woman observed the all-too-familiar tattoo was visible on the woman's arm leading to her throat. The bird and the symbol. The phoenix and the ankh. The publication date was 1877. Nagging sensations pricked at her from within. Familiarity was unlocking closed, dusty doors. The name of the woman in the picture was Diane Bellmore. Who was she? The women's suffrage movement was the backdrop. She could almost recall it. She knew the woman's face all too well.

"She is a life I lived," she whispered, her hand hovering over the article. She looked up. "One of many, many lives. Some were harder than others. I learned from each one though. There was always something to learn—and to teach."

A name flickered in her mind like a candle. Edith Smith. The first female police officer in England. Also her protégé.

Ramona squinted at the picture, lollipop once again at home in her mouth. "She looks white. That means your past lives were different ethnicities. That is so cool. You were—are—like every woman!"

"Well, the Sisters in the Deep Dark did call me the 'woman of many faces,'" she said. In that regard, the twisted albino psychics had not lied. So many faces, so many different lives. Glimpses of yesteryear, different centuries, different visages with the same stormy blue eyes peeking at her around the shadowy corners in her mind. The shadows were receding though. The unveiling would be gradual. She was fortunate it was not like a dam bursting and a tidal wave of past lives crashing into her, carrying her into insanity. Perhaps mental blocks were in place to keep the flow of memory at a steady, incremental pace. She could not tell if they were self-imposed, or if they had been placed there by the crafty and knowing shaman. Pain tugged at her heart. Where was he? He could materialize randomly, it seemed. So much was happening. She could use his counsel.

"So, how did you get all these documents and articles?" Cyrus asked, lifting a quizzical eyebrow at Ramona. "Some of these are really old."

Ramona crunched on her lollipop, finally demolishing it, and tossed the stick in an overstuffed trash receptacle wedged in the corner. "Book café, remember? Plus, when I was younger, I read everything I could get my hands on. Newspapers, advertisements, you name it. If it caught my eye, I read it. My parents encouraged me to excel at everything. Tiger parents, ya know? But I think it kinda backfired when I started reading conspiracy theories and paranormal stuff. They didn't think it was proper for a girl who should have been reading medical books." She rolled her eyes at the memory. "Mother didn't mind as much, but I think she could have stood up for me more. Whatevs."

The woman without a name placed her hand on Ramona's shoulder. "I'm sure your parents are proud of you. In the short time I've known you, I know I am." She squeezed gently.

The punk girl with the bubblegum-hued fauxhawk was stunned, eyes momentarily glassy, before she rushed to fill the silence. "You don't know my parents." Sarcasm dripped like acid from her voice.

Old wounds barely concealed—or healed. Poor child, she thought, touched by Ramona's sensitivity on the matter. "You're right. I don't know them. But I'm blessed to know you."

She gave one final squeeze before withdrawing her hand and indicating the heaps of documentation. She was sure Ramona was grateful for the shift back to the research. "You mentioned earlier how my reincarnation usually precedes some sort of, uh, disaster?"

Ramona looked like she wished she had another lollipop, if only to keep her mouth from opening and closing like a fish on land. Any distraction would have been nice. "Oh yeah, about that. Um, I tracked the last, um, wait what are we calling your, um, returns? Re-emergences?"

"That sounds cool actually," Cyrus said. He was so immersed in an article that he barely looked up. "Remember what the creepy bald girls said about you manifesting? It really had them unnerved."

The nameless woman nodded sagely. It was all coming back to her. The encounter with the Sisters in the Deep Dark seemed like ages ago. "Yes. They said I manifested, and it nearly destroyed their bond. In hindsight, that was not such a bad thing."

Cyrus shuddered. "I can still almost feel them. Like maggots crawling over my skin. Yeah, they were all doom and gloom about your arrival, but I see that as a good thing. They didn't seem that tightly wrapped anyway."

"And yet," she replied, fingering the ankh symbol. It felt surprisingly cool. Curious, she traced a path where it combined with the phoenix. The bird's tail was wrapped around the oval part of the ankh. Warm to the touch. "They seemed to know so much."

"For now!" Ramona declared.

"That's weird," Cyrus added.

Mesmerized, the woman looked at Cyrus. "What is?" She continued to trace the mystical tattoo that ranged in temperature. A faint glow pulsed from it.

"I've never seen it when you weren't in 'angry goddess' mode."

"Angry goddess mode?" There was a note of amusement in her voice.

Cyrus grinned. "Oh yeah. Applicable only when you're creating water portals and controlling water ripped from sinks and pipes!"

"He's got a point!" Ramona agreed.

The immortal woman laughed. "Duly noted."

"But yeah, that's gotta mean something, right?" Cyrus continued. "Maybe it appeared now because you're gaining control."

"And confidence!" Ramona added.

Cyrus cocked his thumb at Ramona. "See? Even the Korean Nancy Drew gets it!"

Ramona scowled in mock anger. "I'm Chinese!"

As Cyrus and Ramona bickered like siblings, the nameless woman found herself thinking about the mystery surrounding her tattoo. Could they be right? Until then, it had only appeared whenever she was in battle mode. Now it had just appeared without provocation. A sign? The old man had given it to her, so anything was possible. Yet another answer that gave birth to a new crop of questions. At that moment, she would have given anything to see his white-dusted skin and frost-colored dreadlocks. Would he heed her call?

Once again, she was met by silence.

Frustrated, she drifted over to a stack of documents. A name stood out to her: Hines Holdings Inc. She lifted an eyebrow. Curiosity got the best of her. She plucked it from the pile. "Ramona? What's this?"

Ramona broke away from her diatribe with her relentless new friend and squinted at the document, despite the hipster glasses. "Oh yeeeeeah. Hines Holdings. They've been popping up whenever there was some clean-up to do."

"What do you mean?"

"Well, they're this privately-owned demolition and construction company. They repair damaged buildings and whatever. Pretty global. Seems legit." Ramona's voice betrayed her true feelings.

"Then why keep tabs on them?"

"Exactly." Cyrus moved in closer to get a better look. "You think it's all connected, don't you?"

Ramona pushed her glasses up and then nodded firmly. "Like I said, they fix stuff. It's what they do. But they were dispatched to some disasters that never made the media."

Cyrus remained silent. Ramona looked at him and then back to the nameless woman, who nodded. "Please, continue."

"A few reporters were dispatched to cover the stories, but something bad always happened to them, and the story was killed, and it never saw print or TV coverage."

"So, how did you know about those?" Cyrus inquired.

"I'm the Korean Nancy Drew, remember?" Ramona teased. "I stumbled onto one case some years ago. I watched it fall into a black hole. So, when there was a minor disturbance, I tracked it closely. The story was dropped, but I hacked into the reporter's computer and retrieved some documents from the hard drive."

"How?" the nameless woman asked, shocked.

Ramona winked mischievously. "Before everything could be

erased, of course. I was in and out." She shrugged. "By minor, I mean volcanic activity on Mount Vesuvius."

Cyrus's draw dropped. "What, wait? Isn't that near—"

"Pompeii," the woman replied. "It destroyed Pompeii."

Ramona, buzzing with excitement, pushed up her glasses and continued. "Yup. It hasn't erupted in a long time, the last time being nineteen forty-four. The files I hacked were another reporter's research. It was uploaded by the guy who disappeared. He was probing the mystery of that eruption and believed there was something paranormal about it. He never got the chance to share it."

Two beings locked in combat on the rim of one of the largest, most dangerous volcanoes in the world. They were lightning fast, trained in the art of battle, and solid blows connected painfully to the face, side, and behind the knees. Both Italian, olive-skinned, attractive, and ready to take out the other. Her scarf blew in the wind. She was fierce and defiant as her booted foot hit the assailant's leg. The snapping of bone was audible. A knife flashed from her boot to give him a bloody grin from ear to ear. Despite the injury to his leg, he dodged the attack—barely. Her nostrils flared, her blue eyes glowing behind her goggles. A phoenix and an ankh burned beneath the sleeve of her bomber jacket. Ash sprinkled their faces like gray snow. The angrier he got, the more the magma boiled...

She blinked as a wave of déjà vu laced with nausea made her stomach queasy. Eyes closed, she felt Cyrus's strong hands on her shoulders, leading her to the bed. She opened her eyes to behold two worried faces staring back.

"I'm okay," she said. "Just got a little dizzy."

"You remembered, didn't you?" Ramona all but squealed.

"Did you?" Cyrus's tone was curious, though it lacked Ramona's excitement. He sat down beside her.

She rubbed her forehead. "I got a visual of a battle taking place atop the volcano. I was there but not there. Well, I was there but in a different body. I was fighting someone. I can barely recall his features, only his deadly intent."

Ramona waited for a moment and then could not resist asking another question. "Do you remember what happened to him?"

A punch was blocked, and an answering punch was delivered. His breathing was ragged. Hers was not. No words were uttered. She sprang up with a kick that sent him careening toward the edge of the gaping, sputtering maw, but then he caught the end of her scarf, and they both fell. Only he managed to grab hold of a rocky crag. She was lost to the bubbling magma below.

"I managed to stop him."

It came to her then—the full story snowing on her much like the ash from the erupting volcano decades earlier. It was his gift, his weapon against hers. He could generate lava, and it was his greatest, twisted desire to recreate the eruption that had destroyed Pompeii centuries earlier. He was close to the source—one of the most dangerous volcanoes on Earth—and he came close to winning. Her gift was nullification. She could suppress the abilities and, in that case, the powers of others. She as a secret agent of the Allies, and he was a free agent of the Axis. A whirlwind romance had left him crippled, incapable of achieving his goal, and she was dead, burned to ash and cinder.

A minor disturbance, indeed.

"Stopped him with my life." As she died, her nullification powers seeped into Mt Vesuvius, thus quelling an eruption that would have eclipsed Pompeii's demise.

Cyrus and Ramona were silent. Baffled. It was a lot to take in.

She rose from the bed, suddenly in need of space. She was starting to get a headache.

"Break?" Cyrus asked, concern darkening his chartreuse eyes. She noted how it knitted his brow and added tension to his shoulders. She was getting good at reading him and he her. And yet . . .

"No. We need to get to the bottom of this," she responded bravely, desperate to quell the doubts that flew around in her stomach. She turned back to Ramona who had been going over more Hines Holding literature. "Anything?"

"Hmm . . . I never . . ." Ramona looked up. "Oh! Sorry. So,

yeah, Hines Holding is actually owned by a cluster of dummy corporations. But it all traces back to one major company. Not sure why I never noticed that before."

The nameless woman and Cyrus looked at the spirited bibliophile with the punk hair. The hairs on the woman's neck began to rise. She braced herself. Ramona gestured pointed to a corporation listed in the document. They huddled closer. "See that name? MalGenPro Labs. They're one of the biggest pharmaceutical companies in the world." Ramona's eyes narrowed into slits, and her lips compressed into a thin line of determination. "Looks like we have a lead, my friends. Let's pursue it, shall we?"

****

Despite the errands she had performed for MalGenPro Labs, particularly at Emmanuel's behest, it was Ariadne's first time visiting the main headquarters at the pleasure of the CEO himself, Amir Moradi. It should have been a great honor, to meet the founder of one of the most prestigious pharmaceutical companies in the world. It ranked somewhere in the top five, but such particulars did not bother her. Yes, details were her thing, but today was different. Today, she was out in the open.

The Spider had deliberately strayed from her web.

A black limo pulled up in front of the skyscraper. Intimidating and futuristic. All monochromatic sleek lines and severe architecture that matched Los Angeles perfectly. Sharp as a razor. Painted lips glistening like a liquid shadow pulled back into a smile. Eyes hidden behind round, minimal baroque sunglasses. She waited patiently as her chauffeur parked and then walked around to let her out. She took his outstretched hand and slid out one long pale leg, which seemed to go on forever before ending in a suede pump with a silver toe. Its twin followed as she stood to her full, spindly height.

"Ma'am?"

Ariadne tucked the envelope clutch in her armpit. "I'll call you. Thank you." She made her way toward the entrance, the wind stirring the long banner of her dark tresses. Her shoes clicked on the marble floor.

A young man wearing black-rimmed glasses and a three-piece suit was eager to greet her at the door. Emmanuel Snow. They went way back. "Ariadne! How was your flight back from Italy?" He put a hand on her back as they entered the MalGenPro Labs HQ.

"Snow." Ariadne slowly removed her shades and blinked her gray eyes at him before she took in the sights, mentally cataloguing them. The information would prove useful later. Details, details. "The flight was uneventful."

Emmanuel knew not to ask about Italy. She was not there for pleasure. "You look nice."

She rolled her eyes. "It's just a black dress with a belt, Emmanuel. You act as if you've never seen one before." The bosom was cut asymmetrically from the left shoulder to her right breast. The smaller portion was a lighter shade of black.

Ariadne heard him chuckle as they entered the glass elevator. Emmanuel had barely pressed the button before the carriage descended in a blur of movement. They passed through level after level, displaying labs and conference rooms. Bright lights. White walls. Black Art Deco furniture. Pleasing to the eye but meant to be observed, not enjoyed. The emissary had a mission, alright. She slid her glasses back on, staring straight ahead as an uncomfortable thought slithered into her head. Better to address it candidly with him now before explaining the mishap to Mr. Moradi. "About the banshee incident . . ."

Emmanuel turned to her, lifted an eyebrow, then resumed staring straight ahead, just like Ariadne. "I wouldn't worry about it. We were all thrown by the vessel's sudden manifestation."

She rolled her tongue over her front teeth. "Hmm . . . I was not thrown off."

He shrugged. "We're only human."

She turned to him with a blank look.

Emmanuel caught it and cleared his throat as the elevator stopped at their floor. The door whisked open. He gestured for her to exit first. "After you."

The Amazon in the designer dress obeyed. Once in the hallway, Emmanuel resumed the lead. She could not let it go. "I've cut loose the other banshees. Too unpredictable. Always whining. Bad for business."

"It's fine, really," Emmanuel assured her as he led her down a corridor leading to double doors protected by armed security guards. "We were all hoping she was disoriented for a simple banshee assassination." He shrugged as he stopped before the doors and nodded to the guards "We were wrong."

She was never wrong. Ariadne was irritably silent. She was glad the former banshee operatives had been injected with a remote-activated cyanide capsule located in their foul mouths. She had to confess, she had taken perverse pleasure in hitting the "on" switch for that overly talkative banshee cosplaying as a nurse.

The doors opened to allow them passage. The room was spacious, set deep in the bowels of the facilities. A massive oval table occupied the center of the room. A plethora of chairs were empty, except for one, its back to them. Slowly, and no doubt for dramatic purpose, it spun around to reveal the man responsible for the company—Amir Moradi, the CEO. The overhead lights gleamed on his bald head. He was the color of mocha—unblemished and handsome. His strong jawline was the envy of lesser men. An impressive build, especially for his age, framed his Armani suit, which was the color of a stormy sky before rain fell. A slow smile crept across his face. When he smiled, the skin folded at the corners of his eyes—the only signs of his esteemed years. When he rose to his feet, Ariadne was quick to notice the slight limp that he worked hard to disguise.

Moradi pumped her hand vigorously and drank in her body in a leering head-to-toe swoop before releasing her hand. "The so-called Spider. You're not what I expected!"

The corner of her lip twitched upward. "I can't say the same thing about you, Mr. Moradi. A pleasure to finally meet you."

The CEO paused ever so briefly, took in her cool demeanor, seemed to reconcile something within himself, nodded, then gestured for her to take a seat. "Charmed. I'm glad we could pry you away from your . . . work in Italy. Our dear Emmanuel seems to have you in his back pocket." He cast a dour side glance at his personal aide.

Emmanuel moved to pull the chair out for Ariadne. Once seated, he gently scooted it closer to the desk. She nodded her thanks and turned her clear gray eyes back to Moradi. "So it would seem, sir. Emmanuel and I attended university together. Old friends and such." She placed her clutch on the table. "Now, I'm told my services are still required. I apologize for the banshee incident. I was not as thorough as I should have been."

Moradi grinned, then shrugged. "Actually, I'm happy with the results. It'll make the vessel's capture all the sweeter. True, her death earlier in the game would have prevented the need for such drastic measures, but it is unfolding all the same. I have waited a long time for this."

Ariadne licked her lips. "Indeed, Mr. Moradi. I was also informed she is traveling with a companion. Is this . . . Cyrus Dhandi still to be apprehended as well?"

The bald businessman pursed his lips, the lines across his forehead growing deeper. "Decision stands. Have you located her? Our psychics are still down."

"I know," she said lightly, crossing one leg over the other, a sliver of light in the dark. "I received your report before I departed. The sisters simply were not ready. And now they're blind, in every sense of the word." She shot him a placating look. "For now, of course. But with that mode of observation temporarily impaired, you called me in to be your eyes out in the field?" Ariadne already knew the answer.

He cleared his throat and brushed invisible dust off his tie. It was clear he was used to being in control. His discomfort was evident, as was his slackening grip on control. He was getting emotional. He would have to do better. Moradi cleared his throat again. "I require all hands on deck for this highly sensitive operation. I will employ any means necessary in the apprehension of the vessel. Your connections are most invaluable."

Her phone vibrated in her clutch. Ariadne offered him an apologetic look before answering it. "Yes? Good. Just in time. Thank you." She ended the call and smiled at both men. It was a smile that would make the average person flinch. It had all the warmth of a snowstorm. "We found her—in San Francisco."

Moradi's eyes lit up like he had just been given the best news of his life. Perhaps it was. "Excellent! Give the word to move in and detain them!"

"Already done, sir. They won't know what hit them."

****

Ramona's studio was a beehive of activity. Her leather jacket hung over the back of her swivel chair as she hunched over her laptop, fingers gliding furiously over the keyboard. The nameless woman sat snuggled in a beanie chair with folders spread across her lap. The only sound was the clicking of the keys and the occasional muttered curse. Ramona's glasses slid down her nose. She did not notice until the nameless woman used her index finger to slide them up. The gesture momentarily brought the tech-savvy bookworm back to reality. She smiled. "I'm just pulling up all known sites. The main headquarters is in LA. Go figure."

The nameless woman looked at the "About Us" page on the website. Amir Moradi was the CEO. A handsome middle-aged man of Middle Eastern descent. "There's something oddly familiar about this man. I can't put my finger on it, but . . ." She tapped the screen with her fingernail. "I'm certain he's the key to all this."

Ramona placed her elbow on her knee, leaned in closer, chin pressed against her balled fist. "Stands to reason, I guess. You can't be bald and good looking and *not* be the super villain. Just look at Lex Luthor."

The nameless woman raised an eyebrow, amused. "The Superman villain?"

Ramona laughed. "Umm . . . yeah!"

She bunched her features in a disbelieving confusion. "You're insane."

"Hey, I like 'em bad and sexy," Ramona replied, leaning back. "Speaking of which, what's going on with Mr. Brooklyn?"

The nameless woman tilted her head. "What do you mean?"

The punk bookkeeper bit her bottom lip. "He seemed a little

weird earlier."

"Ah, yes, indeed, he did. I meant to check on him sooner, but we got so caught up with the research. I think he's outside. I'll go check on him. Be right back."

She found him outside smoking a cigarette, leaning against the wall and doing his best James Dean impression—unintentionally, of course. Amusement and concern warred with each other from within. What was wrong with him? Two cigarette butts lay at his feet. "Cyrus?"

He jerked when he saw her. He hissed under his breath, took one last pull, exhaled a plume of noxious smoke, then tossed the butt to the ground and ground it out under his heel. "You weren't supposed to see that," he said sheepishly.

"Or a great many other things," she replied coolly despite the lingering amusement in her eyes. The constant hustle and bustle of traffic washed over them like a warm summer rain. But to her it was just her and Cyrus. She crossed her arms. "What's going on? You have us worried, my friend."

"Friend…" Cyrus echoed softly, looking everywhere but at her, struggling to settle on her blue eyes. "Do you believe in fate?"

She cocked an eyebrow at him, genuinely perplexed. She was beginning to worry. "I believe I'm living proof of that."

Cyrus chewed his bottom lip. He remained against the wall, but he straightened his leg to stand up. "Yeah. I mean, just look at us. I saved you. You saved me. It was like, I dunno, destined to happen. Like our stories were already written."

She stepped closer. Tension rose between them. "Cyrus?"

He shoved his hands into his pockets. "I spent a lot of time running. I didn't want to be that man anymore. I had to get away, you understand, right?" His voice was strained.

She stood in front of him. The pain in his liquid green eyes was the pain of someone running from his destiny. To her surprise, she placed a hand on his face. Cyrus closed his eyes at her touch. His shoulders sagged, and he let out a shuddering sigh.

"Yes, I do," she said. "We're both running."

"Not anymore."

Before she could reply, an explosion knocked them off

their feet.

Ears ringing, she tried to regain her equilibrium. A cloud of debris hung like a nightmare given semi-tangible form. People cried out. Chaos and panic surged.

"*Cyrus!*"

No response.

"Cyrus!"

She heard muffled talking. Eyes burning, she ran toward his voice. He was pinned beneath a collapsed awning. Grit and blood streaked his forehead. She hugged him tight. "I'll get you out!"

"It's too late," he rasped. Tears threatened to fall. "I didn't know it was them. I didn't know how to tell you. I'm sorry. I'm so sorry!"

"What are you talking about?" she hissed.

"MalGenPro. I didn't know!" Cyrus coughed. He pushed at the twisted debris on his leg like a trapped animal. "It couldn't have been a coincidence. He found us!"

"Us?" The blood roared in her ears. "Cyrus, who's after us?"

As if in answer, they emerged from the smoke like the horseman of the apocalypse. And perhaps they were. High-impact Kevlar body armor. Assault rifles. Dog masks to obscure and protect their features. Their weapons were trained on them. The cries of the wounded served as their introductory theme song.

"My father," he said weakly.

13

Reality refused to align with her equilibrium. She felt as if she was falling again, but she remained rooted to the ground.

His father?

"I don't understand," she sputtered, staring at the barrel of the gun. She turned to Cyrus. He was still pinned, but all signs of resistance were gone. He appeared resigned, defeated. To her surprise, the guns were not trained on him. Only her. What was going on?

"What . . . what are you talking about?"

She shifted.

The guns cocked.

"My father is responsible. These are my father's private security detail, the Vanguard." Cyrus responded, exhaustion and pain shredding his voice to tatters. "We call them his 'dogs of war.' I didn't realize it until it was too late. MalGenPro is his company." Cyrus paused. "It's what I've been running from these past few years."

Betrayal.

An onslaught of emotions smashed into her like a tidal wave. She clenched her fists. The entire time they had been on the run, it was because of her friend, her only friend's father! Hurt and anger, but most of all, rage, battled to dominate her.

"I'm so sorry," she heard him say somewhere in the distance.

The crashing of the waves, the crackling, cicada beat of white static filled every cell, every square inch of her being. She struggled to her feet, which crunched on the scattered debris.

"What the hell?"

Her hair blew upward in an unnatural wind of her own making. The mystical tattoo came to life and glowed in contrast to the grit and dirt that coated her body. Gravity lost meaning. From a place far from her body, she saw herself rise from the ground. Arms outstretched. Pressure building. The spark that held the secrets of her manifested power blinked its cyclopean eye in awareness, awakening from a slumber from which it was glad to be free. Finally. It begged for release.

And she would see to it.

The old man, the shaman, had told her early on that everything was not what it seemed. Where was he now? Had he foreseen this and withheld the information? How could this revelation have been foreseen? And here she was in bed with the enemy. After a fashion, of course.

A phosphorescent spider web of veins flared to life just beneath her skin. It started off cool and refreshing before becoming frigid. She was awakening, and there would be hell to pay.

"Watch out!"

She felt water coursing through the pipes and beneath the streets.

Contact.

She clenched a fist.

Geysers of sewer water burst upward, sending manhole covers airborne. She raised her hand, felt the bond solidify, molding it to her will. She opened her eyes. (When had she closed them?) Cerulean eyes aglow with the promise of swift justice.

"Stop it from attacking!" one of the soldiers yelled.

"It? Man, was that ever the wrong thing to say!" She lashed out with the spray of filthy water. It smashed into several operatives, sending them airborne across the street. "I'm a person!"

Sirens blared in the distance. Irrelevant. She remained a few feet off the ground, a furious goddess in Salvation Army clothing, dispensing punishment to those who wanted to subdue her. She would bring down the entire city if necessary. She was done running. Tired of playing cat and mouse. She would make her last stand. It would all come to an end. And then she would deal with the likes of Cyrus Dhandi!

A scream, a soul-shaking trill of repressed umbrage and the unspoken need to be free sang from within her. It might have even made its way past her lips. She was not sure. Nor did she care. Water blasted everywhere. People screamed in shock and pain. Car alarms blared. She spied a bevy of police cars headed toward her. No matter. She would not be cheated. No longer would she play the fool.

"I will have my vengeance," she hissed in a voice no one would recognize as her own. A wave of her hand procured a wall of water to block off any further interruptions. It was biblical in its presentation.

"No! Don't kill them!"

The voice was clearer. Feminine. Ramona.

The nameless woman turned her ice-blue eyes brimming with a frosty haze toward the young bibliophile. Ramona looked terrified as she took in her friend's terrible beauty. It was an indescribable sight she would recall for her grandchildren in front of a roaring fireplace on the coldest winter day—if she survived this day, that is.

"Remember who you are! Don't let them turn you into a killer! You're so much more than that!"

Guilt and remembrance cut shallow tears into the flesh of her rage. The tattoo scorched her arm as the power inside swelled and raged like a tsunami, barely contained by the weak barrier of her skin, by her flesh and bone. A spider web of blue and orange power glowed all over her body. It was getting easier to call upon her birthright, to summon the gift given to her upon this manifestation. Easier to invoke. Harder to repress. She blinked in rapid succession. "R-Ramona?"

Tears glittered in Ramona's eyes. Tears of sadness and relief. She had gotten through. "Remember who you are!"

Then a bullet punched through the young bookworm's shoulder. The impact spun her against the building's façade. The only sound she made was a gasp of surprise. It was overshadowed by the cry from the nameless woman, the sole survivor of the first tribe, the Wandering Children, who was losing herself in an onrush of indescribable fury and umbrage. Death gleamed in her eyes. The water she controlled would be her sword.

The Vanguard anticipated this and moved in fast. A succession of tranquilizers swarmed at her like angry bees. She erected an obelisk of semi-solid water in time to stop most of the darts, but some bit into her flesh. She grunted and dropped lower but remained airborne. She raised her hand.

"Again!" one of the soldiers shouted.

More darts tore into her.

She landed hard on the street, scraping herself. She staggered to her feet. A banner of tangled locks obscured one glowing, solid-ice blue eye.

"Again!"

Spheres of hard water erupted from her hands as she held them up. They missed their targets by mere inches. Numbness nipped at her limbs.

Her eyes closed for a moment. She heard combat boots pounding on pavement. She opened her eyes. They were near, their intent deadly. Her eyes closed again. Within the next slow blink, they were on her. She feebly raised a hand. Her tattoo glowed dimly.

"That's enough of that!"

A rifle butt found purchase in her face. Crushing pain, and then a blanket of darkness dragged her below.

****

"He doesn't look that special, right?" Emmanuel asked as he observed one of the two captives recently brought in. He removed his glasses and used a cloth to clean them.

"Hmm . . . He's attractive in a scruffy, unkempt way." Ariadne licked her lips, one hand on her hip. "It's what's under the surface that counts, Snow. You know that." She turned to behold the nameless woman. "Case in point."

Emmanuel made a small sound in his throat as he, too, beheld their coveted prize, who was slumped on the floor a high-tech collar wrapped around her neck. "Agreed. Although I must admit I'm just biting my nails for the family reunion between Mr. Moradi and his black sheep of a son."

"They've been estranged for, what, five years now?" Ariadne inquired. "We are in for a most interesting family reunion."

"Um, kinda right here, thanks," Cyrus said, anger and defeat mixed in his tired voice. He had remained quiet on the flight via private jet to MalGenPro Labs headquarters. His injuries had kept him tight and drawn. Yet he gave no outward expression of pain or discomfort. He flashed his smoldering eyes at the well-dressed man, who was close to his age. "Manny! Wish I could say it's nice to see you, but why lie? Still polishing my dad's shoes with your forked tongue?"

Emmanuel flushed and tightened his lips into a thin line. "Your sense of humor hasn't lost its luster. It continues to be a delight, Cyrus. Not to mention an acquired taste. How was the tuna business? Illuminating?"

"It was shrimping, but yeah, it was pretty cool," Cyrus countered. "Felt good to do something on my own. Be my own man. Pretty liberating to break away from being under the thumb of a megalomaniac tyrant. You should try it sometime. But wait. You'd have to grow a pair first. Never mind."

"Because it worked so well for you, my son?" Moradi asked as he entered the foyer flanked by his personal guards. "You two are always bickering. Enough. At least Emmanuel knows his place here. You clearly needed some . . . reminding." He laughed and embraced his son.

Cyrus stood stiff and rigid, his hands handcuffed behind his back. "Dad. You're looking well. Still trying to take over the world?"

Moradi chuckled. It sounded hollow. "One step at a time, Cyrus. But really, Dhandi? That last name?"

Cyrus grimaced, his brow knotted with growing anger. "Dhandi or any surname that wasn't yours, would have served me just fine. I think the distant cousins on Mother's side would have been honored. Maybe even Mother herself."

It happened so fast. Moradi's backhanded slap cranked Cyrus's face sharply to the right. Blood and saliva leaked from his mouth and down his chin. Stunned, Cyrus fell silent. So did everyone else. Everyone but Moradi.

"Prodigal son you may be, but you are still my son, my flesh and blood. You can run as far as you like. You can change your last name a million times. But you will still be a Moradi. My son. My heir."

"Mr. Moradi?" Ariadne ventured.

He broke away from Cyrus, but not before dusting off his shoulders. "You look like crap. We'll get you cleaned up and fed. You and the vessel. Yes, Miss Ariadne?"

"Just Ariadne, sir," she replied, closing the space between them. She looked around before settling her eyes on him once more. "I believe our business is concluded." She offered a manicured hand in parting.

Moradi hesitated, then shook it vigorously. "We couldn't have done this without you. I am most indebted to you. MalGenPro is as well."

A strange smile flexed her black lips. "Indeed, you are, Mr. Moradi. Indeed, you are." She looked back at the vessel. "Such power . . . I hope she survives this experience. Anyway, best of luck, Mr. Moradi. Don't hesitate to call should you need my services." She nodded at Emmanuel.

"Excuse me, sir," Emmanuel said, "but I will see our guest out. Is there anything else before I go?"

Moradi looked down at Ariadne, then let his eyes fall upon his seething, silent son. "I'll take it from here, Snow. Thank you. You are dismissed."

****

She saw pink. Pink hair styled into a Mohawk. No, that was not quite right. The sides were not shaved, which made it a fauxhawk. She also saw a beat-up leather jacket studded with multi-colored buttons and safety pins. Thick-framed black glasses with huge lenses that constantly slid down her nose. A smile. Infectious and full of life.

A bullet.

Smashing into the girl's shoulder and sending her into a wall.

"Ramona!"

The scream ripped from her throat in a raw, abrasive rush. She jerked up, but something kept her restrained. She tugged again. No luck. She opened her eyes and blinked rapidly at the harsh fluorescent lights. She realized her body was restrained to an operating table. Nausea snaked throughout her stomach. She felt sick. But thinking of Ramona, the nerdy girl who loved to read and collect unicorns, made her feel even sicker.

"Ramona? Who's that?" The words were spoken by an unfamiliar voice. It was deep and charismatic. The voice of her captor.

"Where is she?" the nameless woman slurred, her tongue dry and heavy. Her body felt lethargic. "Where's Ramona?"

Her clean-shaven, bald nemesis shrugged. "Repeating the question won't change my answer."

She fell silent. Was he lying? Had Ramona made it out alive? Just thinking about the petite bookstore owner in pain, or worse, intensified her fear. She had to remain positive. To hope for the best. Ramona had to be alive.

Another person came to mind. Someone she wished to kill but whom she found herself thinking about, nonetheless. "Cyrus," she whispered without thinking. She instantly regretted it.

Her captor smiled broadly. "You care for my son, don't you? He's always had that effect on women. Probably the only thing he inherited from me." He chuckled darkly. "Don't fret over him. He's safe. I would worry more about you."

She narrowed her eyes, bristling. "I take it you're the emissary."

"When I'm not approving business proposals or having power lunches, yes, I go by that name." He moved in closer, his eyes like dark storm clouds gathering. Unreadable but ominous. "A fitting moniker, really. It means one with a special mission. A sacred one."

"How thrilling for you." When had she started channeling Cyrus and Ramona? "Am I supposed to be impressed?"

"No, you're supposed to remember. You don't remember me?"

She opened her mouth to spew more sarcasm but then squinted and let the question roll over her. Something was vaguely familiar about him, now that he mentioned it. "I'm sorry, but no."

"You're a liar," Moradi said flatly. "You came to us that night many decades ago. You came to us, and everything changed for the first time."

"You must have me confused with someone else," she said unconvincingly, avoiding his burning gaze. He had the intensity of a fanatic.

With a speed seemingly impossible for someone his age, Moradi was suddenly in front of her. His eyes gleaming, he jabbed at the flesh on the left side of her body. A tingling sensation sparkled beneath her skin. The faint outline of her tattoo glowed dimly before he removed his finger. Then it faded away. "Ah, it responded to my touch, my old friend. If there was ever any doubt in my heart, it's gone now. I know who you are. What you are."

Doubt, much like his intrusive touch, traced a path through her mind. Her soul. "I don't ... I don't remember."

Moradi smiled again. "For once, I get to be the storyteller. Once upon a time ..."

****

It was 1961. Rural Afghanistan, Khewa to be exact. Some thirty years before war left bombed-out buildings and streets riddled with craters and landmarks. The only dirt road in the center of town had always been the natives' focal point, their marketplace. That was the road she took as she emerged from the shadowy, mountainous regions of eastern Afghanistan. With silent eyes, she took in the sad state of affairs—the mud huts that lined the streets with the most basic wares. She felt the stagnant vibes of the changeless place through the soles of her feet. Khewa was known to be a crossroads for those migrating from place to place. No one stayed unless they had been born there. She had a long way to go. She would rest there for a while.

A farmhouse caught her eye. Her stomach growled. She

pressed a hand to it before making her way to the door. She hoped the occupants would answer.

After a few knocks, she heard scrambling on the other side of the door, followed by raised voices. The door swung open to reveal a young boy, no older than five years of age. He gaped at the hooded visitor, his little mouth forming an "O" of surprise and awe.

"Amir!" A pregnant woman wearing a chador, a large scarf wrapped around her head, rounded the corner brandishing a ladle. "What did I tell you abo—" her voice caught in her throat when she saw the strange woman standing in her doorway. "My apologies. We shall talk later, Amir. Can I help you?"

The nameless woman's stomach twisted at the sight of the ladle and the smell of soup cooking. She was so hungry. "I'm sorry for the intrusion. I was passing through. I saw your home and hoped I could trouble you for some food."

The expectant mother smiled warmly in return. Amir, who had hidden behind his mother, peeked around shyly. "You're just in time," the woman said. "I just finished making dinner. You're welcome to join us."

As they sat at the small modest table, names were exchanged. The woman's name was Arezu. They were just getting by, since the untimely death of her husband Vakil. She spent most days outside carrying water and tending to their meager crops. Little Amir served as her errand boy. He wished to be older so he could help more.

"My little man wants to be just like his father," Arezu said, laughing as she poured soup into the visitor's bowl. "But my little prince can only do so much." There was a touch of sadness in her voice.

"I can do more!" Amir exclaimed, pounding his small fists on the table and crossing his arms petulantly. "But you won't let me."

"Now, Amir, be reasonable," his mother cajoled. She coughed. Amir looked up, worried. Arezu wiped her mouth on the back of her hand. "Your leg prevents you from doing anything too hard. I won't allow it."

"What's wrong with his leg?" the visitor asked, genuinely curious. She sipped her soup, enjoying the feel of carrots and potatoes in her mouth, along with bits of stringy meat.

"Nothing!" Amir declared.

Arezu shot him a warning look. "My son injured himself while playing with some of the other boys in the mountains. He fell and broke his leg. It never healed right."

The drifter stood up. "May I see it?"

Suspicion flickered in Arezu's eyes. "What?"

The visitor pulled back the hood to reveal startling cerulean eyes. "I believe I was brought to you for a reason, Arezu. I can help you and your family."

Arezu frowned in disbelief and waddled over to pull her son from his seat. He struggled in vain. "What are you?" she asked.

"A healer. I can help, if you let me."

The pregnant widow held one hand protectively over her swollen abdomen and the other over Amir. She moved her lips to say something, but no words came out. She looked at Amir, who returned her gaze hopefully. She knew he sometimes had pain when walking. If there was anything the stranger could do to help him . . .

"Alright." Arezu kissed the top of Amir's head and coaxed him toward her. "Don't make me regret this."

"You won't," the visitor replied as she effortlessly picked up the boy and set him on a cot. She rolled up his pant leg and saw the lump of bone pressed tight against his skin. She touched it. He flinched. She smiled at him, which seemed to ease the tension in his small body. She felt her mystical tattoo awaken, the stirring of power sending tingles throughout her body. She had the gift of healing, and she let it flow from her like thick, unspooling honey. It made her feel light and airborne, and it tasted of liquid sunshine. Sometimes, to mend the spirit, one had to mend the body.

Amir sighed in sweet relief as the bone aligned itself. He was still aglow with the hazy amber radiance of healing power. His smile made her travels up to that point worth it. He would walk again without pain. For all his days.

"There . . ." She rose to her feet, a bit wobbly.

"You . . . healed him," Arezu said incredulously. "You healed my boy."

The drifter nodded and placed a hand on her forehead. "May I rest?"

"For as long as you wish."

The next couple of weeks were the best in Amir's life. He was able to play with the other boys again and help his mother in the fields. Truthfully, he assisted their newfound friend, who insisted on doing the chores. Arezu protested despite being so close to giving birth to her second child. Amir took to calling the stranger "Hadyah," which means "gift" in Arabic. He was besotted with her, and she adored him, her little helper.

"Where are you from, Hadyah?" Amir asked one day when they were outside milking a scrawny goat. His mother was inside, preparing supper.

She paused mid-task and smiled up at the boy. He was vibrant, fully healed, no trace of his infirmity. "From the first tribe. I was one of the Wandering Children. We are mostly forgotten now, but I alone still live."

Enraptured, Amir lowered himself until he rocked on the back of his heels. "Wandering Children? Like me?"

She laughed. "No, not quite. It was one of our many names. We were a magical tribe that came from the heart of Africa. We were the first to migrate, to explore. We journeyed to the west. Our gods followed. We were so full of life and wonder. And magic." She winked at him.

Amir beamed with excitement. "So, where are they now?"

Her eyes darkened. "They are only memory now. Long gone. My special soul allows me to live on forever."

Amir considered this for a moment. "It seems lonely."

She opened her mouth to respond, but then they heard a call from Arezu. Dinner was ready. Secretly, she was relieved. "Let's bring the milk to your mother."

The days leading to the delivery were difficult for Arezu. The birthing process was even harder. She was in labor for over seventy-two hours. The blood. There was so much blood. The stranger taxed her healing powers to keep Arezu relatively comfortable. There were no doctors, and the local midwife lived in the city of Jalalabad. It was all on her.

Arezu's skin was clammy despite the sweat that glistened on it. She was delirious as she called for Vakil and sang to Amir. Once when she beheld the visitor, she clasped her hand feverishly. "Aleema! Most exalted one! I see your radiance now. My angel!"

The blue-eyed healer did not pull away. "You're almost there. I see the head."

Arezu screamed and then pushed. "Save my children. Don't let anything happen to them..."

Tears glittered in the stranger's eyes. There was so much blood. Too much. She and Arezu were weak. She was vaguely aware of Amir in the background, staring in mute horror, pale and fragile. Arezu was not going to make it. The child would die too. They both knew it. Her own strength was dangerously depleted, her grip on her power tenuous. She could only save one life.

"You will be fine. Just give me one more push, and then you can rest."

A tear slid down the side of her face and into her hair. They shared a look. They both knew a choice must be made. Arezu nodded. Grabbing the sides of the bed, Arezu birthed her small child in one shuddering push. It was the last of her strength as a new stream of blood flowed. A newborn's wail filled the air.

"My... my little prince," Arezu said, reaching for Amir. "You grow up and leave this dead place. Be something. Watch out... for your... little..."

Silence.

Arezu's eyes were still open, but the soul that had animated them a moment earlier was gone. With a trembling hand, the visitor lowered the dead woman's eyelids and then cradled the squalling newborn, still covered in afterbirth. "Rest well, sister. Your daughter will know that you sacrificed your life for her and her big brother."

A slight tremor shook Amir's frame. He trembled as he stared numbly at his mother's cooling form. It took an eternity for him to make his way to her and kiss her cheek. With heaving shoulders, he crawled into the bed with her. The stranger held the newborn to her bosom. She knew she should comfort the boy, but she remained rooted and transfixed. It brought a painful memory of her own parents leaving this realm altogether. So many thousands of years ago, yet the pain was still there, a universal ache felt by all. The same universal pain expressed by a little boy weeping silently in his deceased mother's cold embrace.

A few nights later, the visitor awoke with a start. Cold dread washed over her. She strained to listen. Silence. It was too quiet. She slid out of bed. Her heart pounded. Her instinct told her to check on the baby, whom they had named Sapidah. She opened the door. It creaked on ancient hinges.

"Sapidah?"

Silence.

Mouth dry, she entered the room and lit a small candle. In the darkness, she saw Amir hunched over the crib, his back was to her.

"Amir? What's going on? Did your sister wake you?"

Amir turned around slowly, clutching a pillow. His dark eyes were glassy. His bottom lip trembled. "I did a bad thing. A very bad thing."

"What . . . What did you do to Sapidah?" She could not hear past the roar in her ears.

Fat tears rolled down his cheeks. "She was crying. I tried to stop her from crying. She wouldn't stop. I got so mad. And I . . . and I . . ."

"You what?" her reply came out hoarse. She already knew.

"I put the pillow on her face to stop her from crying. She finally did." Amir looked back at the dead infant, hidden from view.

Before she realized it, she was on him. She grabbed him by his shoulders and gave him a violent shake. He cried out in alarm and tried to push her off. Every ounce of frustration, sadness, and rage erupted from her in that moment. She slapped him hard. She raised her hand to strike him again but then paused. He was a child, but he had killed an infant, and he had to be punished.

"H-Hadyah?"

Her tattoo flared to life. Her eyes smoldered in a blue glow, the only illumination in the dim room. Power whispered throughout her body. Bled into every cell. Gave strength where it was needed. Her task was clear. "Don't call me that. Ever again."

She mimed pulling something from him. He cried out as he staggered back. Tendrils of amber energy snaked out of the shaking child. He dropped to one knee as the wispy strands of magic that had restored his leg were recalled back into her.

An eye for an eye. A life for a life. The ankh pulsed a wintry blue that flowed into the orange glow of the phoenix as power was reclaimed. She cast a luminous eye toward the crib. No life pulsed from it. A pang of indescribable emptiness pierced her core. The child that she had nursed following her mother's death had joined her mother in the afterlife. The childless mother. She gathered her shawl and wrapped it around her head.

"Don't leave me," Amir begged, tugging at the hem of her dress as he lay on the floor. "Don't leave me here with them."

Her unfeeling eyes bore into his red-rimmed orbs. "I was never here."

When she left, she never turned back. Her heart was stone to the wails of the murderous child.

****

"You killed your baby sister," she choked, tears streaming down her face. "You killed your baby sister!"

Amir Moradi dabbed at the corner of his eyes, cleared his throat, and then stood up and turned his back to her. "I was so angry after Mother died. I blamed Sapidah; it's true. She was crying that night. I tried to help, but then I remembered what she did to my beautiful mother."

She struggled against her restraints. "You killed an innocent child!"

"No!" He whirled around, eyes burning like black coals. "It was an accident. Besides, no one is truly innocent, Hadyah."

She burned with animosity. "I told you once a long time ago not to call me that again. You lost that right when you smothered Sapidah."

A muscle twitched along his jaw. "And were you any better for leaving me, alone and frightened? Broken?"

"It was the best I could do." Doubt tried to worm its way in, but she suppressed it, scowling at him. "You survived."

"But not the memory," he replied, gesturing dramatically. "That memory gave me hope. You wanted me to forget you, but, how could I? You came into our lives one night and changed everything. You restored my health but took my mother. Then you stole back my health. You took back my vitality, and you almost took my will to live. I found something better though."

Disgusted, she raised her eyebrow. "You were meant to be more, but somehow, you are less."

Moradi stared at her soberly. "And you were like a mother to me. I lost two mothers in the span of weeks. But I knew if I kept searching for you, you would appear. That's what you do, right? You always return." A haunting smile dredged from the pits of insanity flashed across his face. "The vessel has returned for the first time. Initially, I wanted you dead because I was angry. I was going to dissect your corpse and pull forth every delicious, bloody secret that has kept you alive for so long and then take back what you stole from me. But that all changed when Cyrus entered the picture. Talk about fate!"

Cyrus. His own son! She had been drawn to him for a reason, but why? Had her innate power recognized the blood relation? It was a question that would have to be answered another time. "What are you going to do to him?"

Her former charge looked askance and then chuckled. "Oh, don't worry. I won't smother him with a pillow, if that's what you're thinking. But I also can't continue to abide by his reckless, damaging nature. He will be punished severely. You will get to see him one last time before you become the basis for my next wave of pharmaceutical products."

Moradi turned to leave.

"Amir?"

"Yes, my dear Hadyah?"

"Was it worth it? Is this what your mother asked of you with her dying breath? Is this the life she envisioned for you?"

For the first time, he looked like the little boy she had met over fifty years earlier—lost but determined. "Probably not, but it was the life you made possible."

****

He had meant to cut her up and make biodegradable beauty products from her remains. Moradi had grandiose plans for soaps, body washes, face creams, and even lipstick. After all, she was the key to everlasting life. It would have been too fantastic to believe, but she had heard it directly from Moradi himself. His scientists had all but confirmed it in terse conversations conducted in small huddles. As she was wheeled into an observation room, she heard them discuss the usage of nanite technology to keep her subdued and her hydrokinetic powers in check. *That explains me being physically powerless with Amir*, she thought sourly, feeling lethargic and vaguely angry. She was shackled but on a genetic level. A slave to another and not her memories.

She seethed.

"As seen here in her recent attack on the Vanguard forces, she has considerable control over water." The words were spoken by a scientist with silver-rimmed glasses and a brunette bun who was clutching a tablet. She was the lead scientist. Her metallic name tag read "Dr. Astrid Cromwell." She tapped on the screen, and a hologram of the nameless woman's anatomy materialized. The other scientists moved closer as small rectangular boxes of high-definition news footage showed her displaying her water-manipulating abilities against the Vanguard in San Francisco.

"In just the last seventy-two hours, we have seen her gain more maturity with its various applications. Aggressively so. Look at this." A new video popped up showing grainy footage of the Cairns hospital banshee situation. "See how she summoned water from the IV bag first? As you know, the contents mostly consist of electrolyte solutions, potassium chloride, etcetera. This variation of her power shows a broader inclusion of liquid manipulation, not just water. We will test her limits with various exercises. Then we'll move on to the final phase—dissection. She is not to be in the general vicinity of water or any other water-based liquids, understood?"

The cluster of lab-coat-wearing scientists nodded before breaking up to perform their various tasks. The nameless woman could only roll her tired eyes in their direction as they transferred her from the gurney to an operating table. They buzzed around her, attaching nodes to her arms and legs.

Somewhere during the process, they had removed her tattered clothing and replaced it with a simple hospital gown. Her tangled locks rested on the thin pillow. Her tattoo was nowhere in sight, absorbed into her flesh due to the dulling effects of the tiny robots nullifying her gift from within. The magic suppressed her gift more effectively than she would liked. She hated feeling powerless.

"But are you really helpless, my little sparrow?"

She gasped and craned her neck toward the all-too-familiar voice. "How are you here? What took you so long?"

The shaman emerged from the darkest shadows of the laboratory. The harsh glare of the overhead lights seemed to make his cracked white face paint glow. Long-limbed and magical, he was a throwback to a time where science had no place. He was an aberration in that room of cold, mechanical equipment; an anachronism. Much like her. They were magic. They were more.

"What took me so long? You didn't need me."

"Are you kidding me?" she snapped, straining to rise, to no avail. "I could have used your help numerous times!"

He chuckled, then looked around. "No, you didn't. Not really. From beyond the veil, I watched you. Watched you come into your power. You still can."

Frustration bubbled in her stomach. "They injected me with tiny robots!"

The old man laughed. "Tiny robots? Truly this is an age of wonders."

She narrowed her eyes. "I'm glad you find this funny."

"It's the little things, Daughter of Eternity." The old man's chuckle died in his throat. He turned his inky black eyes, offset by the chalky white that coated his dark flesh. "Enough of this foolishness. Now, rise."

"I can't!"

"You must. Now, do it."

She closed her eyes, angry tears beading the corners. She zeroed in on the nanites locking her body down. They resisted her advances. Her tattoo remained invisible and dormant. "I can't . . . it's . . . fighting me."

He looked at her, the light reflecting off his shadow-cloaked eyes. "Then fight back."

Something occurred to her. She had to ask him. "I saw you die. How are you still here? How are you still alive?"

The shaman laughed. "My child, who says I am? Who says I'm even here?" He pointed at the scientists, who seemed oblivious to their interaction. "I could be a fever dream. A figment of your imagination. Or perhaps a living memory."

Tears flowed down her cheeks. He had answered a lingering question she already knew in her heart. As if to give credence to her suspicions, she tried to reach for him. Face somber, her old mentor walked over to the table, close enough to touch. She inched a finger close to his. It passed through, as if it was not there. Her head snapped up to stare into his eyes. They appeared wet and shiny.

"I'm not here, little sparrow. Not in the physical sense, and not in the other senses that matter. When your mind fragmented at the time of your last death, you gave life to an old memory of yours. Your power shaped and changed it. You gave sentience to a part of your subconscious. You chose my visage."

Realization crashed into her like a freight train, knocking the air from her lungs. The entire time the old man had been a part of her own mind, brought to life. The last thread connecting her to the life before her endless stream of lives was no more than a fleeting sensation, déjà vu on two legs. Since the start of her new life, she recalled their solo conversations that no one else seemed to notice. It made sense. Such loneliness on a cosmic scale. It was almost enough to make her curl into a ball and give in to whatever dark, twisted fate Moradi had in store for her.

"Rise, girl."

"No. You're not real."

"Rise. You must."

"It's over."

"Not yet."

"I can't."

"If not for yourself, then what of the fisherman?"

Her eyes snapped open. Cyrus! "Where is he? Is he in danger?"

The old man turned his serious eyes on her. "You heard what your former ward said. You know what he intends to do."

Panic braided with soul-searing fury arched her back. She could not allow Moradi to destroy his son, her friend. Cyrus had not known who was pursuing them. And even if he had, why should he be blamed for his father's sins? The nanites struggled to keep her subdued. She pushed back. She was magic, the oldest science since creation. And she had been playing the survival game for a long, long time.

She took control of herself. Memory, mind, body, and soul. She fused them together into a single entity and reclaimed her body from the technology's sorcery. The ancient power that whispered in every nook and cranny of her soul awakened and recognized the alien interlopers within. Her inner voice spoke, and the nanites were destroyed. She rose from the bed. Shouts from the scientists buzzed like insects in her ears. They ran from her. A technician, husky and bald, summoned security. She knelt beside him and grabbed a fistful of his shirt.

"Where's Cyrus?"

The technician squirmed in her grip. His name tag read "Schwartzwalder." His lips trembled in the forest of his beard. "Please, don't hurt me!"

"Don't give me a reason to," she growled. "I repeat: Where is Cyrus Dhandi?"

"H-he's in room two fifteen. Uh-oh." He looked down as a dark stain darkened his white pants.

"Disgusting." She ripped off his lanyard and exited the room.

Alarms blared, and red lights flashed down the long white corridors. "This is place is state of the art, right?" she said to herself. She cracked her knuckles. "Computer, provide me with a directory."

Suddenly, a green holographic map of the building blipped

into existence. Her angry blue eyes narrowed when they fell upon Cyrus's location. He was close by.

Her legs pumped as she recalled racing alongside gazelles in the veld. The thrill of the hunt soared in her. The phoenix trilled from within, blinking its avian eye. It was all so familiar. She had traded tribal garments for a hospital gown. It made no difference. She exhaled as she skidded to a stop in front of Room 215. She swiped the badge and entered.

It took her a moment to realize what she was looking at. When her mind finally comprehended, she charged in roaring the battle cry of the first tribe. Cyrus was strapped to an elevated chair, his bloody mouth open as his own father pulled out his teeth. Cyrus had no control of his legs, which spasmed and jerked. Three teeth lay in a pool of saliva and blood on a metal tray.

His sleeves rolled up, Moradi turned toward the intrusion. He was sweating. Emotion as raw and bloody as Cyrus's extracted teeth scorched her soul and gave voice to an unspoken rage that rose to the surface, wet and pulsating, alive and terrible. Her claws raked across Moradi's face, followed by a sequence of punches. Moradi held up his arm to block her, but she was fury in the form of a woman.

"He's mine! He's under my protection!"

Moradi bellowed as he smashed his elbow into her face. The impact sent her careening into the opposite wall. A shadowy haze emanated from him, licking at him like black flames. "No! He is mine to deal with! My blood! And his blood I will take! He was meant to take over when his brother died, and he will!"

Dazed, she brushed her hair from her eyes. She tasted blood in her mouth. Brother? What was Moradi rambling about? She tried to regain her composure, but the emissary was on her. His hands enclosed around her throat and began to squeeze.

"You made me obsessed with perfection and beauty. I don't know how I did it, but I found the perfect wife, Kamelah. She reminded me of you. She was at my side throughout medical school and when I came to America to build my dream. We became the American Dream. She bore me two sons. Amir the second and Cyrus, my heirs to all that I have built."

She began to lose strength as he gained his. Her legs felt wobbly.

Moradi, still aglow with otherworldly energy, looked down at her, oddly serene as tears mixed with the blood from the cuts on his face. "Amir, my golden child, was meant to take over my legacy. He knew this. He was my pride and joy. But Cyrus?" He barked out a laugh that held neither mirth nor humor. "Always in trouble at school. Stealing and running with the wrong crowd. The bane of my existence. But then my Amir died in a skiing accident, and I was left with . . . that." He nodded toward his only surviving son, whom he had been torturing.

Her eyes watered. The life was being crushed from her.

The Vanguard, the so-called dogs of war, were suddenly at the door. They stopped as they rounded the corridor and aimed their guns at her.

"Boss?" the leader of the unit asked, his gun trained on her.

"Can't you see I'm in the middle of something?" Moradi roared. He spun his head toward the Vanguard, his eyes pitch black, and pointed at the door. "Get out! Go! Now!"

They lingered for a moment before retreating around the corner. The alarms still rang in their ears.

Moradi turned his gaze back to her and smiled. "See, Hadyah? It's all about power. You just gotta have a pair."

She had tried to summon the water from somewhere in the room, but she had no such luck. Moradi had it sealed off. But she was not without her resources. "Yes, Amir, I agree . . ." It took the last of her strength to drive her knee firmly between his legs.

Contact!

Moradi let out a strangled whimper and hunched over, releasing her as he clutched his groin. The corona of dark energy that surrounded him wavered and dimmed. She grabbed his shoulders, shoved him against the wall, and shook him. "Look at what you've done! What have you become?"

He looked up at her, his eyes black orbs of night, his lips bloody and cracked. "I am the emissary," he whispered. "I am an envoy of dark tidings, my Hadyah. The serpent is come."

Her tattoo flared to life. How was that possible? There was no water to manipulate. Then another part of her recognized something in the flickering blackness that consumed the soul of the child she had left decades earlier. She refocused on the task at hand. At that moment, she was struck by a stark realization. The human body was composed almost entirely of water!

Her eyes of blue fire pulsed with terrible purpose. With a dramatic gesture, she twisted her fingers, brought her elbows in, and thrust her hands upward. As if in slow motion, tendrils of water were ripped from Moradi's pores.

He screamed as a nimbus of water tinged in blood hovered around his form, which was becoming increasingly withered.

She began to float. The supernatural strength borrowed from his black energy was no more. He lifted a feeble hand as if to ward her off, but how could an ant stop a goddess?

"S-stop!"

She whipped her head around and glared at the source of the voice: Cyrus. He had managed to free one hand from his restraints.

"D-don't d-do this. You're better than h-him."

She continued to float in the air, immersed in her element. Her hair had transformed into a wavering, blue-tinged halo of water. The bright colors of the phoenix and ankh tattoo beamed from her neck. Whispers of the past chanted softly in her ears. Past lives blossomed in the garden of her memory. Her soul was a stone tablet with all the secrets of her past selves inscribed upon it in glowing script. She was the woman of many faces. The woman with no name. Eternity's Daughter. The childless mother. She was . . . her.

She turned back to her dying prey. "He has to pay. For killing his sister. For coming after me. For harming you." She clenched her fist to underline her point. Moradi flailed like a dying fish on land.

A shaking hand touched her elbow. She turned back and narrowed her eyes. "Don't try to stop me, Cyrus. Don't share his fate."

Cyrus smiled, blood crusted around his mouth and chin. "Determined for me to leave you so soon?"

She blinked, and a shudder rippled through her body. Her feet touched the ground. "Cyrus? Cyrus I ..." She blinked back tears and returned her gaze to Moradi. "I'm not a killer. I'm not a killer. I'm not a killer." The halo of water and blood was reabsorbed back into Moradi's withered body. His flesh regained its normal luster, and his breathing evened out. He remained on the floor.

Cyrus staggered as he caught her when she collapsed heavily against him. They sat on the floor, locked together, her arms wrapped around his waist. Cyrus winced but did not push her off. He buried his face into her hair. "I'm always here for you no matter what. You can't shake me."

She pulled back and stared in his tired eyes. "What did you just say?"

Cyrus looked at her, confused. "What?"

She backed away. "Are you . . . him?"

Cyrus squinted, perplexed. "Him? Who?"

She tried to feel if the lingering magic was still there. It was so familiar. But then it was gone. Not even a wisp of it remained.

14

"This hospital food sucks so bad," Ramona griped. She was propped against the pillows in her hospital bed, her shoulder bandaged. She looked miserable.

The nameless woman responded with a chuckle as she held up a Goodie Box bag. The instant joy in Ramona's face made her laugh. "I know what you mean. So, Cyrus and I managed to snag some of your favorite food on the way here. Stella says hi, by the way."

Squealing, Ramona tried to clap in glee, but then she remembered her bandaged arm. She winced. "Almost forgot why I was here."

Mirroring her discomfort, the nameless woman's laughter died in her throat. "I'm sorry this happened to you. I never intended for you to get hurt. Or Cyrus." She looked at them.

Cyrus had remained quiet since they returned to San Francisco. They had met no resistance when they hobbled out. Moradi had retreated somewhere in the vast headquarters to lick his wounds. For some reason, Emmanuel had ensured the battle-weary duo underwent state-of-the-art medical treatment for their various injuries sustained that day and since the start of the journey, speeding up the healing process substantially. Cyrus was suspicious as he sat there being poked and prodded and bandaged. He refused to ingest anything. So did she.

As they were leaving, Emmanuel met them in the foyer. She and Cyrus wore matching white T-shirts and pants. The company logo was stamped on the right breast. Cyrus was tense, his shoulders bunched together. She looked at Emmanuel. "If, for any reason, you attempt to sabotage us . . ." she threatened in a low voice.

Emmanuel held up his hands in submission. "No, we here at MalGenPro Labs only want to help. We're sorry—Mr. Moradi is very sorry—that things came down to this."

Cyrus sneered. "Well, at least we can all agree on that, Snow. My father is a pretty sorry individual. But it stops here. He's done pursuing us. Got it?"

Emmanuel had the grace to look humble and sheepish. "We were . . . overzealous in the pursuit of the vessel. Considering recent events, we have decided to pursue less, uh, destructive avenues of research." Emmanuel cleared his throat. "In fact, the board has decided to fly you back to San Francisco, where your friend, Ramona Li, is recuperating in a local hospital. Rest assured her medical expenses have been paid for."

Shocked silence wafted between them like a sour wind. Cyrus narrowed his eyes. "No more games, Emmanuel. No tricks."

"No games. No tricks, Cyrus," The bespectacled personal aide reassured him. "We are sorry."

"You really were made for this, weren't you?" Cyrus said.

Emmanuel raised his eyebrows. "Excuse me?"

"All this. You've always been spineless. A coward. But look at you now. A one-thousand-dollar suit. Expensive glasses. That snake smile. You're in your element, Snow."

"Thank you, Cyrus."

Now they were back in San Francisco with a truly courageous friend, who had taken a bullet for a woman who was immortal, timeless. The irony was not lost on them. They sat around Ramona's bed devouring the greasy hamburgers and milkshakes. The Jell-O on the food stray lay neglected and ignored. They ate in silence for the most part. The vessel, the fisherman, and the scribe.

Ramona had begun to doze off when Cyrus looked at the nameless woman. "Can I see you outside for a moment?"

Her stomach did a flip flop. She knew what he wanted to do talk about. An unbidden return to the recent memory of them sharing a life-shaking embrace near his father's recovering form.

She could still feel the strength in his arms despite his injuries as he held her. The raw moment of vulnerability had opened something. Something familiar. Questions had bugged her during their trip back. If she could be reincarnated, then why not him? Could Cyrus be the reincarnation of the warrior who had betrayed her? She hated to ask such questions, but that did not stop them from assaulting her every waking moment until she closed her eyes.

They were silent, each lost in their own maelstrom of thoughts as they exited the hospital. Cyrus' hands were stuffed inside his pockets. She crossed her arms. It was their first time alone together since before the Vanguard arrived and caused a substantial amount of property damage to get her. She supposed Hines Holdings would be cleaning up the mess. A ghost of a smirk flitted across her lips.

"So, I started smoking again," Cyrus revealed by way of conversation. He appeared frustrated by the announcement. "I know it's wrong, but it's been stressful since all this happened."

She averted her gaze, her heart heavy with the revelation. "You mean since I came into your life. I hate that you're smoking again. It'll kill you."

"No, no, no, I don't blame you!" Cyrus replied, holding up his hands. "I just don't handle stress well, and with my dad being the cause of . . . well . . . I needed something to do. Plus, he's the reason I'm going to need some dental work."

Anger, wet and fluid, coursed through her veins at the thought of Cyrus's recent torture at his father's hands. Tears threatened to spill from her burning eyes. "Your father still has so much to answer for. I wanted so badly to kill him. To hurt him for hurting you. He's hurt so many people and has taken so many lives along the way."

Little Sapidah came to mind, the spectral infant of so many years ago.

Cyrus nodded tersely, avoiding eye contact. "He's always been a monster. My brother and I lived in fear of him, even before he drove our mother crazy. Literally."

Kamelah. Moradi had mentioned her during his brief, brutal

battle with her. Kamelah was the mysteriously absent mother of the Moradi sons and heirs to his fortune. Where was she now?

An old hurt and darkness trickled into Cyrus's eyes. "Mom couldn't take it. She was so fragile and timid. And Dad . . . was Dad. She protected us from his rages when she could. Especially when we were children. But she found her escape with prescription pills. She became hooked, tried to flee with us, but Dad tracked her down like a dog. After that, something inside her broke. She gave up. Amir became Dad's shadow, and I became a hot mess. She was institutionalized when I was sixteen."

She turned her glittering eyes on him and reached for his hand. "I'm so sorry."

He nodded quickly, cleared his throat, then clasped her hand. "Don't be. You got him to leave us alone. That's more than I could ever do."

She looked at him, truly looked at him. The tall, bruised, attractive man from a place of a beating, merciless sun during the day and cold, unforgiving nights, swirling sands, camel caravans, exotic spices, and resolute, unshakable faith rooted deep in the land. His eyes were the color of sparkling green water, cool and inviting. His scruff had thickened since that first fateful day aboard *Peaches*. A wiry strength was evident in the set of his shoulders despite his injuries. And that lazy, lopsided grin that complemented his eyes, his come-hither eyes.

The memory of their embrace swam to the forefront of her mind. The trace of dark, paranormal power that hung over Moradi. The way Cyrus said a phrase she had heard so many times before her life changed for eternity. Could her greatest nemesis have been reincarnated in the form of her first self-sacrificing friend? Could fate be that cruel? Could she be that trusting?

The long-hidden secrets of her shattered identity had been reconnected, those questions finally answered at the cost of near-death experiences. Bonds of trust had been forged in those purifying flames. Everything should have been set right. She should be able to lower her walls and embrace her protector with the New York accent. She should be able to let down her guard and start a new life in this modern world. There was much to experience, to love, to drink in and add those defining patches into the tapestry of a new and glorious life, a life without running, a life meant to be lived to the fullest. Not alone but hand in hand with her only two friends.

She should have been able to do it. And yet something unanswered remained.

"Why are you pushing me away?" Cyrus asked in a small voice. She heard the hurt in it. His eyes appeared wide and too bright, but not like his father's crazed eyes. Cyrus was a man in pain. A man who had run for so long, thought he found stability, and found it slowly breaking away like a receding wave off the moonlit shore.

He squeezed her hand, then placed it over his beating heart. He swallowed hard, lowered his gaze, then forced himself to stare into her uncertain eyes. "I won't hurt you. I never will. You know that, right?"

Her words were lost in her throat. Tension drained from her shoulders. She would have to trust him. To learn from her mistakes. She would not break another heart or be careless with another life. She would not be a monster. But she still needed to be honest with herself. To come to grips with her recent questions. To be sure.

"Do you trust me?" His eyes were pleading, pools of swirling green intensity. His heartbeat increased. Fear and uncertainty labored his breathing.

"*Nothing is what it seems*," an old, wisecracking man had said to her early in her life-altering journey.

Some things simply were.

"Honestly? I'm learning to, Cyrus," she replied, her hand still atop his surging heart. He placed his other hand over hers. The gesture brought a smile to her lips.

"I finally found the answers I was looking for," she said, "but I still need to sort out so much. I also have much to answer for, my friend." Shame and guilt at what she had done to his father recently and over fifty years earlier haunted her.

Cyrus was quiet for a moment. He licked his lips, appeared to make peace with something internally, then blessed her with his trademark grin. "Okay, it's a start. I won't beat a dead horse. But if you need me..."

She smiled and moved in to hug him. "You're here, I know. Thank you."

She could tell he did not want to break the embrace, but he finally let go. Reluctance seemed to settle uneasily over him. "Any time." He cleared his throat and stepped away. "Hey, let's see if Ramona has burned down the hospital room yet, yeah?"

She chuckled, absently rubbing her clavicle and nodded. "Yes, we both know she can't be left alone for long."

She felt a tangible drop in tension between them. He seemed more at ease, less pensive. Yet there was something else. It hung between them. She also felt better, but suspicions nagged her. She would have to proceed with caution. She hated feeling that way. She wanted everything to be perfect. But life never was.

"What took you guys so long?" Ramona demanded, brandishing the television remote. While they were gone, she had attacked the Jell-O. Not a trace of it remained. She indicated the television, which was mounted to the wall opposite her bed. "You guys missed the opening credits to the Golden Girls!"

Cyrus bowed and shook his head.

The nameless woman frowned in confusion. "What are the Golden Girls?"

Ramona gasped. "You don't know about the Golden Girls? You don't know about 'Thank you for being a friend'?"

Cyrus burst out laughing.

"I'm afraid, I don't, sorry," the nameless woman confessed. "What's it about?"

"Zip it, Cyrus!" Ramona said sitting up. "It's about four elderly women living together in Miami. Naturally, hilarity and hijinks ensue. It's so freakin' funny."

The nameless woman raised an eyebrow.

Ramona gushed on. "And Dorothy is, like, the bestest."

"You are sorely mistaken, our little emo bookworm," Cyrus interjected. "The best one on the show is Sophia. Don't deny her awesomeness."

Ramona sputtered. "Are you dense? Wait, you're smoking

again, right? So, listen here, Puff the Magic Dragon, we both know Dorothy has the best one-liners through and through. Case closed. Next?"

Cyrus grabbed for the remote control, but despite her injury, Ramona was faster. "Of course, the old spinster would have the best lines."

"They're all old! And another thing..."

The two friends went back and forth hotly debating the classic 1980s TV show as the nameless woman looked on, thoroughly amused. Cyrus and Ramona bickered like old friends. On the outside looking in, it would hard to believe they had met only days before. She could tell they cared for each other and that their newfound friendship would endure for a lifetime. She smiled. It felt good to see their relationship develop.

A prickling sensation started in the back of her mind. A memory whispered to her, rising from the vastness of her soul. "Guys?"

"So what? Dorothy was super cool. Everyone wanted to be her!"

"What? Bitter and angry?"

"That's not true! Dorothy told it like was!"

"Guys," she tried again, a realization blossoming and new. Her bottom lip trembled.

"Dorothy hated life!"

"How dare you?"

"Guys!"

They both whipped their heads toward her. "What?"

"I remember . . . my name!"

Ramona dropped the remote control. It clanked as it hit the floor. Cyrus's jaw nearly hit the floor along with it.

The nameless woman was nameless no more. Happy tears spilled from her overflowing aquamarine eyes. The mass of natural curls seemed to bounce as she closed the distance between them and held their hands. Her breathing sped up. The final piece was laid bare before her and, within seconds, her friends.

"My name is . . . Safronia."

Epilogue 1

The panoramic view of Los Angeles did nothing for him. The glittering, urban skyline could not lift his spirits. After a long day at work, the highly successful CEO would often sit at his desk, seat swiveled around to face the "City of Angels" below. It reminded him of how far he managed to climb. He was no longer a mere mortal scaling Mount Olympus. He was the king of Mount Olympus, ruler of it all. But tonight was different. Tonight, he was troubled.

Tonight, Amir Moradi sat in despair.

He stared down at his big hands. Somehow, he could see the blood on them. He imagined how trusting his baby sister had been a moment before the pillow stole her little life. He remembered killing his friend over a minor dispute, a blow to the head. They had been hustling their wares in the market. Moradi perceived that he had been swindled. So, he took a rock and bashed in Abdul's skull. His only friend. He remembered his hands on his beautiful wife, Kamelah, that first time. She had quelled the rage within him. In the same breath, she had added to it despite her uncanny resemblance to his betraying Hadyah, his first unrequited love. Those hands that once showed her love and compassion balled into fists and struck her whenever he was upset. He watched her wither away and then descend into medicated limbo, followed by the impenetrable depths of insanity. His hands had done that. Those same hands had held his crying sons after they were born. Such loud squealing things! But so beautiful, his seed given flesh. Amir, his firstborn, was to take over one day. Then fate stole him, taking him into the realm of death. His other son, Cyrus, who looked so much like his mother, had been right to run from him especially after the beatings. His hands had caused so much pain. But they had also built so much.

Then he thought of her. How he hated her. It was her fault. She had made him into this monster.

Moradi heard the chittering of locusts from somewhere in his dark office, telltale signs of a great reckoning. He broke out into a cold sweat. *No, no, no not now*, Amir thought, fear stealing into his limbs and locking them in place. His leg throbbed. He tensed. It only throbbed when the Dark Other was near. Whispers floated from the shadows, speaking of great and terrible things, malevolent and enticing.

The shadows seemed to lengthen and thicken. They twisted and turned. Tendrils snaked along the floor and crept toward the ceiling, ebony fingers grasping for anything to corrupt. A new presence entered the room, seeming to fill every nook of the biggest office in the MalGenPro Labs facility. The pressure built and built, taking all life with it, poisoning it. His lame leg throbbed. Pain shot up and reached out, much like the shadows. It was her fault. He had been spared the crippling pain before she returned it. Then she had done the same with his life! She was no better than him. They were two sides of the same damned coin.

"Amir…" A deep voice rolled in honeyed thunder, crashing like a tidal wave with jellyfish to sting him all over his exposed flesh.

He knew the voice all too well. A slight tremor shook his body. His shaking hands gripped the armrests of his chair. He forced himself to stare out the window at the twinkling city. Why had he not left early? Why had he remained? Truthfully, there was nowhere he could run. Not from the serpent.

"My emissary in disgrace…"

In the window's reflection, Amir spotted twin golden eyes in a sea of darkness. They blinked. Total blackness. When the tawny eyes reopened, Moradi saw a masculine shape begin to dissolve from the deepest part of the shadow, sliding from the umbra. He bowed his head, then turned slowly to face his nocturnal caller.

"Y-yes, my Dark Lord?"

Those hellish eyes blinked once more. "Have you ever wanted for anything, my emissary?"

"No, my lord. You have seen to my every want, my every need."

"Indeed." The man who seemed almost entirely in shadow approached Moradi's desk. His features were chiseled and breathtakingly handsome. His hair was hard to make out in the wealth of shadow. It was cut close to the scalp. His barrel chest flowed into a well-defined abdomen before it blended into wispy darkness. An ancient lion-tooth necklace rose and fell as the ancient entity breathed. He seemed semi-tangible, but the promise of dark tidings emanating from him like an oozing, angry wound was quite real.

Moradi willed himself to turn around, but a tentacle the color of nightfall prevented him from doing so. He was not fit to gaze upon the Serpent's burning visage. As if to prove a point, his lame leg stiffened as a new surge of pain burned through it. It took everything in him not to cry out and show weakness in the presence of the ancient spirit.

"She left you in the small rundown shack you called home. She left you to fend for yourself and bury the infant child whom you slew." His voice undulated with each word, twisting and turning like a snake in the grass, overflowing with thunderous malice. "A broken child crying for a dead mother and for a surrogate mother who turned her back on you. Do you remember how desolate you felt?"

The memory was always close to the surface. It was the last time he had felt truly helpless. It was one of the chief factors that drove him even to this day. The answer was obvious, and yet he replied with a soft, defeated, "Yes."

The living shadows encircled his chair and slowly turned him around. Finally, their eyes met. It never got easier. Moradi wanted nothing more than to jump out of his skin and through that window.

Every.

Time.

Moradi saw him full on. Once again, he was that little boy in fearful awe of something greater than himself. The dark one, the aggressor, was masculine beauty carved from living shadow and smoke. Strong and muscular. His eyes were the color of molten gold set in a face of pitch darkness. Perhaps in his first life, when he was human, he would have been able to bed and wed anyone he deemed worthy.

"Do you also remember who found you? Do you remember who took you into their warm embrace?"

How could Moradi forget? "It was you, my lord." Moradi remembered how the shadows in his home had grown and stretched before those demonic eyes blinked in the dark. The tendrils were so cold, enshrouding him and pulling him close. Moradi had been so desperate for any kind of comfort he welcomed it gladly. The darkness that had been a man had hugged him and assured him everything would be fine. Promised him greatness.

"You were blinded by her false light, but I gave you the flickering flame of pure darkness," he continued, as the shifting shadows began to burn. "In the dark, a trained warrior can see and can hunt his game. Did my borrowed power not give you all you desired? Did it not give your twisted leg strength?"

Moradi hungered for the black flames. It was the only thing that could sooth his internal and external pain. But his master was fickle. The power had been loaned to him and could be taken back at a moment's notice. This was the reason Moradi strove to excel. He wanted to be worthy of him and his addictive power. Only his master could restore what she had taken away. He bit his bottom lip in need.

The Serpent smiled, white teeth flashing like a blade in the moonlight. "I saved you from your broken, little life, a life that was over before it truly began. I carried you in my arms and have done so ever since." Moradi detected a subtle accent in his tone that harkened back to the original sable sons of the Dark Continent.

The disgraced CEO hung his head in shame. It was not often that he was subjected to this type of humiliation. Throughout his years of excelling in the medical industry and then creating his own pharmaceutical company, he had relied heavily on the support and power the serpent had given him. His hands hovered over his shaking leg. Sweat glistened on his forehead. But this was different. Something was building, like the calm before a disastrous storm darkened the horizon. Moradi needed to curry favor. "My lord, forgive me. You have been my lord since I was a child!"

A barbed claw made of darkness raked across his cheek. Moradi cried out. He opened his eyes to see blood dripping on the floor. A shudder rippled through his body.

The ancient spirit rose higher, inky blackness oozing from beneath his exposed, flat stomach like an octopus discharging ink from its flailing tentacles. He seemed to fill every space, claim every corner, and still loom before the terrified businessman. The lion tooth gleamed around his neck, the light catching the yellowed enamel. Tribal trinkets adorned his bulging arms, not entirely lost in the smooth ebony flesh. "You were supposed to kill her. You were not to give her a chance to marshal the power locked in her cursed, eternal soul. Your hubris was your undoing. Over what? Your misbegotten son!"

Moradi did not lift his head to look into his master's burning eyes. He had handled things all wrong. He had wanted to humiliate her and steal all her secrets to improve his business. Moradi had let emotion rob him of the gift of her death. It was all his master ever wanted. He had waited so long. "I was wrong. When I found out my son was traveling with our immortal foe I—"

The malevolent entity struck Moradi again. "She is *my* immortal foe. Not yours. Do not presume to think you are on our level. You were a means to an end. And now I see that is at an end!"

"He's my son!" Moradi shouted, his voice shrill and cracked, immobilized in his seat. "I had to spare him. I had to!"

The ancient evil hissed and lifted the shaking man into the air. "Your flesh is of no use to me. It matters not whether he lives or dies. It matters not whether you live or die."

"I gave my life to you! You promised me salvation!" Moradi cried, tears and snot streaming down his face.

"And I gave it to you," was all the serpent said before snapping Moradi's neck and tossing his lifeless body to the floor.

Slowly, he lowered himself beside the man who had once

been CEO of MalGenPro Labs. His impressive form began to take more of a humanoid shape. The wisps and streamers of night were sucked back in. Amber hued power trailed from his eyes. The office slowly resumed its normal state of illumination at that hour. It was only dusk, after all. The tendrils of darkness resolved into a loincloth above two strong, sturdy legs. An ancient spear materialized in his hand. On the dark flesh of his arm burned a glowing tattoo depicting a snake entwined upon an ankh.

"But you mortals do not last forever. Specks of dust lost in the winds of time. Only she and I will remain for eternity."

He turned from the shattered, cooling corpse and walked over to the window that granted him the breathtaking beauty of Los Angeles. He clasped his hands behind his back and smiled wickedly, the corners of his eyes crinkling. The smile reached his eyes. Those laughing eyes. "She can run from me, but she can never shake or lose me. I will always find her."

Epilogue 2

From on high, they watched, mostly in silence. Whatever council surged in their hearts and minds, they kept it from flowing past their lips. They had been watching for a long time, but time had no meaning in that place. The passing of several centuries was but a blink. Humans and their petty woes, trials, and tribulations were a constant source of amusement. So predictable and yet so intriguing. Changeless, and yet sometimes they could surprise! They could stand apart from the cattle they bedded, the cattle they slew. The special ones stood out and unknowingly garnered attention from those watching from a baobab tree.

The realm below was no longer mist and swamp, shapeless and without life. They saw that, long ago, thanks to one of their number, who had stepped outside the proverbial box, the world below was a different beast entirely. No longer chaos but simply chaotic in its own twisted, beautiful way. Tiny insects crawling over a rock. Never once looking up. Well, not in their direction anyway. "Too many cooks in the kitchen," as humans might say. They went about their mundane business unaware they were being observed from a place in the sky.

Mortals thought they had free will, but it was an illusion. The future was not theirs but the will of something greater and perhaps less special. Their unspectacular destinies and fates were already written. The seer had written this down before humankind worked the Earth. However, two unique humans had a rare story that went back ages. Ribbons of light and black floating and crisscrossing through the centuries. The only uncertainty were the future stories. They remained unwritten and hidden. This fact intrigued the observers most of all.

The immortal woman, forever smiling the same, eternal smile from different faces, blue eyes twinkling no matter the flesh she wore. Different bodies, always varying in skin hues, so many different colors and complexions. First, the wild-haired dark-skinned beauty that was the chieftain's daughter. The shaman's apprentice. Innocent and playful. She was the best of the first tribe, for she was simply . . . her. They had chosen her well through their proxy, the shaman. A fierce fire burned in her core, an intense thirst for life that set her apart from the others. She had been chosen because she was life. The woman named Safronia.

Light could not exist without darkness. There could be no life without death. And if there was ever an antithesis to the woman of many faces, it was the dark other, the serpent, the aggressor. In life, he was bold, arrogant, and warlike; the first to lead the charge into battle with opposing tribes or give chase to the gazelle, often in conflict with another predator, the lion. On occasion, lions also fell beneath his spear or hunting knife. Even to this day, he wore the ancient lion-tooth necklace around his neck. Since that fateful day, when he laid waste to the ailing survivors of the first tribe, he had grown into a dark, twisted thing born of scorn and unspeakable rage. He became the stuff of nightmares. Only her true and final death would quell the eternal rage in his ancient soul. The man was named Zuberi.

The sky dwellers were most enraptured with these two ill-fated children of the first people. Their story was one of depthless pain and physical reunion, time after time. Safronia and Zuberi, the only survivors of the tribe that arguably started all human life, were still caught in a game of cat and mouse, the products of choices made passionately before most civilizations were born. They flitted and flirted like birds crossing each other's path borne on the winds of time and change. They were immortal but not changeless. Lifetime after lifetime, they evolved and achieved the next step toward rebirth. Their story was still unfolding. And the elders watched. Always they would watch. But now was the time for commentary.

"She has finally rediscovered her name," one figure said, a sly smile upon his lips. "It was there all along. Took her long enough."

"It happened when it was destined to happen. It was always fated after the most recent events she was forced to endure," another voice replied, wise and precognitive.

"Trickery notwithstanding, she stayed true to the course," a third wise and known voice said from the shifting light and dark. "Her destiny will not be denied no matter what obstacles befall her."

"Even the pestilence that took the life of her people could not stop her," yet another voice agreed. "And that plague of my making should have been enough to wipe out the entire first tribe."

The ancient beings of indescribable power murmured as they peered into the realm of mortals.

Esu, the trickster at the crossroads and messenger between humankind and deity.

Orunmilá, the deity blessed with divinity, foresight, and wisdom.

Ori, the metaphysical embodiment of intuition and destiny.

Babalú-Ayé, the deity of disease, illness, and healing.

They were but a handful of the Yoruba Orishas who had watched Safronia, the enigmatic beauty, throughout the ages, throughout her lives. They had much vested interest in this woman who wore many faces but kept the same heart. But not all rooted for her. Some thought her dark counterpart, Zuberi, would win. And had he?

"The girl does not stand a chance, my brothers," Esu proclaimed. "There is no way she will be ready for him when he chooses to show himself."

"He is right," Babalú-Ayé agreed. "Despite her manifested power, she is fragile and unprepared for what is to come. The human flesh can endure only so much."

"See?" Esu teased. "And this is coming from the one who set that fateful pestilence upon that village. He knows the limitations of the human body."

"But not of their spirit," Ori interjected, ire in his voice. "The race is not yet run. She no longer gestates in the waiting realm. She is no longer in need of a new life, for she has found it. Fate has found her. She is back on Earth for a glorious purpose, a preordained mission. You must take heed, for there is more to come."

Esu laughed, the sound mischievous and grating. "Oh? Is that so?"

"It is," Orunmilá replied, "for this is only the beginning . . . of Her."

Acknowledgements

They say, "third time is the charm," but in this situation, I am soooo okay with it being the second time! I am grateful to God for giving me this second chance to get my debut novel back out there for you guys. Thank you so much for your patience and support. And thank you for this gift.

I do not know where I would be if I did not have this ability to share my words, my stories, with you. I thank my siblings, Toni and Malcolm, for helping birth my passion for storytelling. We would world build and craft stories daily in a fictional town called "Gloving Gluff."

Granddaddy, thank you for always encouraging me to read and for taking me to the comic book shop every Sunday. I will never forget that. Thank you for shaping the author I would become.

Charles Gibson, THANK YOU. Your motivation and tough love regarding the return of *Her* was so necessary! There were so many days I wanted to say, "Eff it!" and you would be like, "Oh no you won't, sir!"

And a warm thank you to my teachers, Marc Nagelberg, Patricia Harris, and June Torns. Thank you for always believing in me and for seeing more inside the quiet child you met in your classrooms.

Beth Kattleman, a.k.a. Mizz K, the bestest librarian and dear friend I could ever ask for. Thank you for, well, everything.

To my roleplaying buddies who stood by me for almost 20 years as I worked on my craft. You guys remember how rough my writing used to be!

And a very special thank you to my friends and fans who helped make this re-release possible! Dear ones such as Elisa Rodriguez, Mekka Williams, Wes Sims, Joan Daymon, Olutisin Taylor, Joy Stephens, Kofi "Old Man Logan," Artis Manning, Tom and Kitty Havrish, Christy Nelson, Melanie Nelson, and so many others saw my Indiegogo crowdfunding campaign and did not hesitate to donate. I did not forget you, Paul Robinson (R.I.P). You ALL made this possible.

Last, but certainly not least, thank you, Kevin Miller. You have been such an incredible editor and typesetter. It has been a long road, and you have been there since I decided to tweak my novel. Thank you for your patience and guidance!

Made in the USA
Middletown, DE
22 July 2024